D1342377

Darkness Becomes Her

KELLY KEATON

SIMON AND SCHUSTER

A **simon pulse** book

First published in Great Britain in 2011 by Simon & Schuster UK Ltd,
1st Floor, 222 Gray's Inn Road, London WC1X 8HB
A CBS COMPANY

Published in the USA in 2011 by Simon Pulse,
an imprint of Simon & Schuster Children's Division, New York.

A CIP catalogue record for this book is available
from the British Library

ISBN 978-0-85707-145-3

10 9 8 7 6 5 4 3 2 1

Printed in the UK by CPI Cox & Wyman, Reading, Berkshire RG1 8EX

Darkness
Becomes Her

One

UNDER THE CAFETERIA TABLE, MY RIGHT KNEE BOUNCED LIKE A jackhammer possessed. Adrenaline snaked through my limbs, urging me to bolt, to hightail it out of Rocquemore House and never look back.

Deep breaths.

If I didn't get my act together and calm down, I'd start hyperventilating and embarrass the shit out of myself. Not a good thing, especially when I was sitting in an insane asylum with rooms to spare.

"Are you sure you want to do this, Miss Selkirk?"

"It's Ari. And, yes, Dr. Giroux." I gave the man seated across from me an encouraging nod. "I didn't come all this way to give up now. I want to know." What I wanted was to get this over with and do something, *anything*, with my hands, but instead I laid them flat on the tabletop. Very still. Very calm.

A reluctant breath blew through the doctor's thin, sun-cracked lips as he fixed me with an *I'm sorry, sweetheart, you asked for it* look. He opened the file in his hand, clearing his throat. "I wasn't working here at the time, but let's see. . . ." He flipped through a few pages. "After your mother gave you up to social services, she spent the remainder of her life here at Rocquemore." His fingers fidgeted with the file. "Self-admitted," he went on. "Was here six months and eighteen days. Committed suicide on the eve of her twenty-first birthday."

An inhale lodged in my throat.

Oh hell. I hadn't expected *that*.

The news left my mind numb. It completely shredded the mental list of questions I'd practiced and prepared for.

Over the years, I'd thought of every possible reason why my mother had given me up. I even explored the idea that she might've passed away sometime during the last thirteen years. But suicide? *Yeah, dumbass, you didn't think of that one.* A long string of curses flew through my mind, and I wanted to bang my forehead against the table—maybe it would help drive home the news.

I'd been given to the state of Louisiana just after my fourth birthday, and six months later, my mother was dead. All those years thinking of her, wondering what she looked like, what she was doing, wondering if she thought of the little girl she left behind, when all this time she was six feet under and not *doing* or *thinking* a goddamn thing.

My chest expanded with a scream I couldn't voice. I stared hard at my hands, my short fingernails like shiny black beetles against the white composite surface of the table. I resisted the urge to curl them under and dig into the laminate, to feel the skin pull away from the nails, to feel something other than the grief squeezing and burning my chest.

"Okay," I said, regrouping. "So, what exactly was wrong with her?" The question was like tar on my tongue and made my face hot. I removed my hands and placed them under the table on my thighs, rubbing my sweaty palms against my jeans.

"Schizophrenia. Delusions—well, *delusion*."

"Just one?"

He opened the file and pretended to scan the page. The guy seemed nervous as hell to tell me, and I couldn't blame him. Who'd want to tell a teenage girl that her mom was so whacked-out that she'd killed herself?

Pink dots bloomed on his cheeks. "Says here"—his throat worked with a hard swallow—"it was snakes . . . claimed snakes were trying to poke through her head, that she could feel them growing and moving under her scalp. On several occasions, she scratched her head bloody. Tried to dig them out with a butter knife stolen from the cafeteria. Nothing the doctors did or gave her could convince her it was all in her mind."

The image coiled around my spine and sent a shiver straight to the back of my neck. I *hated* snakes.

Dr. Giroux closed the file, hurrying to offer whatever comfort he could. "It's important to remember, back then a lot of folks went through post-traumatic stress. . . . You were too young to remember, but—"

"I remember some." How could I forget? Fleeing with hundreds of thousands of people as two Category Four hurricanes, one after another, destroyed New Orleans and the entire southern half of the state. No one was prepared. And no one went back. Even now, thirteen years later, no one in their right mind ventured past The Rim.

Dr. Giroux gave me a sad smile. "Then I don't need to tell you why your mother came here."

"No."

"There were so many cases," he went on sadly, eyes unfocused, and I wondered if he was even talking to me now. "Psychosis, fear of drowning, watching loved ones die. And the snakes, the snakes that were pushed out of the swamps and inland with the floodwaters . . . Your mother probably experienced some horrible real-life event that led to her delusion."

Images of the hurricanes and their aftermath clicked through my mind like a slide projector, images I hardly thought of anymore. I shot to my feet, needing air, needing to get the hell out of this creepy place surrounded by swamps, moss, and gnarly, weeping trees. I wanted to shake my body like a maniac, to throw off the images crawling all over my skin. But instead, I forced myself to remain still, drew in a deep breath, and then tugged the end of my black T-shirt down, clearing my throat. "Thank you, Dr. Giroux, for speaking with me so late. I should probably get going."

I pivoted slowly and made for the door, not knowing where I was going or what I'd do next, only knowing that in order to leave I had to put one foot in front of the other.

"Don't you want her things?" Dr. Giroux asked. My foot paused midstride. "Technically they're yours now." My stomach did a sickening wave as I turned. "I believe there's a box in the storage room. I'll go get it. Please"—he gestured to the bench— "it'll just take a second."

Bench. Sit. *Good idea.* I slumped on the edge of the bench, rested my elbows on my knees, and turned in my toes, staring at the V between my feet until Dr. Giroux hurried back with a faded brown shoe box.

I expected it to be heavier and was surprised, and a little disappointed, by its lightness. "Thanks. Oh, one more thing ... Was my mother buried around here?"

"No. She was buried in Greece."

I did a double take. "Like small-town-in-America Greece, or . . . ?"

Dr. Giroux smiled, shoved his hands into his pockets, and rocked back on his heels. "Nope. The real thing. Some family came and claimed the body. Like I said, I wasn't working here at the time, but perhaps you could track information through the coroner's office; who signed for her, that sort of thing."

Family.

That word was so alien, so unreal, that I wasn't even sure I'd heard him right. Family. Hope stirred in the center of my chest, light and airy and ready to break into a Disney song complete with adorable bluebirds and singing squirrels.

No. It's too soon for that. One thing at a time.

I glanced down at the box, putting a lid on the hope—I'd been let down too many times to give in to the feeling—wondering what other shocking news I'd uncover tonight.

"Take care, Miss Selkirk."

I paused for a second, watching the doctor head for a group of patients sitting near the bay window, before leaving through the tall double doors. Every step out of the rundown mansion/mental hospital to the car parked out front took me further into the past. My mother's horrible ordeal. My life as a ward of the state. Daughter of an unwed teenage mother who'd killed herself.

Fucking great. Just great.

The soles of my boots crunched across the gravel, echoing over the constant song of crickets and katydids, the occasional splash of water, and the call of bullfrogs. It might be winter to the rest of the country, but January in the deep South was still warm and humid. I gripped the box tighter, trying to see beyond the moss-draped live oaks and cypress trees and into the deepest, darkest shadows of the swampy lake. But a wall of blackness prevented me, a wall that—I blinked—seemed to waver.

But it was just tears rising to the surface.

I could barely breathe. I never expected this . . . *hurt*. I never expected to actually learn what had happened to her. After a quick swipe at the wet corners of my eyes, I set the box on the passenger seat of the car and then drove down the lonely winding road to Covington, Louisiana, and back to something resembling civilization.

Covington hovered on The Rim, the boundary between the land of the forsaken and the rest of the country; a border town with a Holiday Inn Express.

The box stayed on the hotel bed while I kicked off my boots, shrugged out of my old jeans, and jerked the tee over my head. I'd taken a shower that morning, but after my trip to the hospital, I needed to wash off the cloud of depression and the thick film of southern humidity that clung to my skin.

In the bathroom, I turned on the shower and began untying

the thin black ribbon around my neck, making sure not to let my favorite amulet—a platinum crescent moon—slip off the end. The crescent moon has always been my favorite sight in the sky, especially on a clear cold night when it's surrounded by twinkling stars. I love it so much, I had a tiny black crescent tattooed below the corner of my right eye, on the highest rise of my cheekbone— my early high school graduation present to myself. The tattoo reminded me of where I came from, my birthplace. The Crescent City. New Orleans.

But those were old names. Now it was known as New 2, a grand, decaying, lost city that refused to be swept away with the tide. A privately owned city and a beacon, a sanctuary for misfits and things that went bump in the night, or so they said.

Standing in front of the long hotel mirror in my black bra and panties, I leaned closer to my reflection and touched the small black moon, thinking of the mother I'd never really known, the mother who *could've* had the same teal-colored eyes as the ones staring back at me in the mirror, or the same hair. . . .

I sighed, straightened, and reached behind my head to unwind the tight bun at the nape of my neck.

Unnatural. Bizarre. Fucked up.

I'd used all those words and more to describe the thick coil that unwound and fell behind my shoulders, the ends brushing the small of my back. Parted in the middle. All one length. So light in color, it looked silver in the moonlight. My hair. The bane of my existence. Full. Glossy. And so straight it looked like it had taken an army of hairdressers wielding hot irons to get it that way. But it was all natural.

No. Unnatural.

Another tired exhale escaped my lips. I gave up trying a long time ago.

When I'd first realized—back when I was about seven or so—that my hair attracted the *wrong* sort of attention from some of the foster men and boys in my life, I tried everything to get rid of it. Cut it. Dyed it. Shaved it. I'd even lifted hydrochloric acid from the science lab in seventh grade, filled the sink, and then dunked my hair into the solution. It burned my hair into oblivion, but a few days later it was back to the same length, the same color, the same everything. Just like always.

So I hid it the best I could; buns, braids, hats. And I wore enough black, had accumulated enough attitude throughout my teenage years that most guys respected my no's when I said them. And if they didn't, well, I'd learned how to deal with that, too. My current foster parents, Bruce and Casey Sanderson, were both bail bondsmen, which meant they put up the bail money so defendants could avoid jail time until their court appearance. And if the person didn't show for their appointment with the judge, we hunted them down and brought them back to jurisdiction so we weren't stuck footing the bill. Thanks to Bruce and Casey, I could operate six different firearms, drop a two-hundred-pound asshole to the floor in three seconds, and cuff a perp with one hand tied behind my back.

And they called it "family time."

My hazy reflection smiled back at me. The Sandersons were pretty decent, decent enough to let a seventeen-year-old borrow their car and go in search of her past. Casey had been a foster kid too, so she understood my need to know. She knew I had to do this alone. I wished I'd gotten placed with them from the beginning. A snort blew through my nose. Yeah, and if wishes were dollars, I'd be Bill Gates.

Steam filled the bathroom. I knew what I was doing. Avoiding. Classic Ari MO. If I didn't take a shower, I wouldn't get out, put on my pj's, and then open the damn box. "Just get it over with, you big wuss." I stripped off the last of my clothes.

Thirty minutes later, after my fingertips were wrinkled and the air was so saturated with steam it was hard to breathe, I dried off and dressed in my favorite pair of old plaid boxers and a thin cotton tank. Once my wet hair was twisted back into a knot and a pair of fuzzy socks pulled on my forever-cold feet, I sat cross-legged in the middle of the king-size bed.

The box just sat there. In front of me.

My eyes squinted. Goose bumps sprouted on my arms and thighs. My blood pressure rose—I knew it by the way my chest tightened into a painful, anxious knot.

Stop being such a baby!

It was just a dumb box. Just my past.

I settled myself and lifted the lid, pulling the box closer and peering inside to find a few letters and a couple of small jewelry boxes.

Not enough in there to contain an entire life story. No doubt I'd have more questions from this than answers—that's usually how my search went. Already disheartened, I reached inside and grabbed the plain white envelope on top of the pile, flipping it over to see my name scrawled in blue ink.

Aristanae.

My breath left me in an astonished rush. *Holy hell.* My mother had written to me.

It took a moment for it to sink in. I trailed my thumb over the flowing cursive letters with shaky fingers and then opened the envelope and unfolded the single sheet of notebook paper.

My dearest, beautiful Ari,

If you are reading this now, then I know you have found me. I had hoped and prayed that you wouldn't. I am sorry for leaving you, and that sounds so inadequate, I know, but there was no other way. Soon you will understand why, and I'm sorry for that, too. But for now, assuming you were given this box by those at Rocquemore, you must run. Stay away from New Orleans, and away from those who can identify you. How I wish I could save you. My heart aches, knowing you will face what I have faced. I love you so much, Ari. And I am sorry. For everything.

I'm not crazy. Trust me. Please, baby girl, just RUN.

Momma

Spooked, I jumped off the bed and dropped the letter as though it burned. "What the hell?"

Fear made my heart pound like thunder and the fine hairs on my skin lift as though electrified. I went to the window and peeked through the blinds to look one floor down at my car in the back lot. Nothing unusual. I rubbed my hands down my arms and then paced, biting my left pinkie nail.

I stared at the open letter again, with the small cursive script. *I'm not crazy. Trust me. Please, baby girl.*

Baby girl. Baby girl.

I had only a handful of fuzzy memories left, but those words . . . I could almost hear my mother speaking those words. Soft. Loving. A smile in her voice. It was a real memory, I realized, not one of the thousand I'd made up over the years. An ache squeezed my heart, and the dull pain of an oncoming headache began behind my left eye.

All these years . . . It wasn't fair!

A rush of adrenaline pushed against my rib cage and raced down my arm, but instead of screaming and punching the wall like I wanted to, I bit my bottom lip hard and made a tight fist.

No. Forget it.

It was pointless to go down the Life's Not Fair road. Been there before. Lesson learned. That kind of hurt served no purpose.

With a groan, I threw the letter back into the box, shoved the lid on, and then got dressed. Once my things were secured in my backpack, I grabbed the box. My mother hadn't spoken to me in thirteen years and this letter from the grave was telling me to run, to get to safety. Whatever was going on, I felt to the marrow of my bones that something wasn't right. Maybe I was just spooked and paranoid after what I'd learned from Dr. Giroux.

And maybe, I thought, as my suspicious mind kicked into high gear, my mother hadn't committed suicide after all.

TWO

I HURRIED DOWN TO THE CHECKOUT COUNTER, HANDED IN MY key, and then headed out the back exit to my car. The streetlamp buzzed, flickering occasionally, highlighting the haze that hung low in the air. Frogs and crickets chanted from beyond the chain-link fence that separated the parking area from the overgrown, watery ditch that ran the length of the lot.

With every step, I became increasingly skeptical and felt increasingly stupid. What the hell was I doing fleeing because of some letter? And what was in New 2 that I needed to avoid? Answers to my past? Why I was a freak of nature? More info on my mother's life?

My mother might've warned me, but she probably never envisioned that her only daughter would turn out to be a part-time bail bondsperson. I could handle New 2 and anything else that came my way.

Once again, I put the box on the passenger seat and my oversize backpack on the floorboard. My fingers flexed on the steering wheel, and I sat in the driver's seat for a long time, hating my indecision.

I'd learned about Rocquemore House and the place of my birth, New Orleans, before leaving Memphis. Bruce and Casey had been cool with lending me one of their vehicles, knowing I was more mature and responsible than most adults. I was seventeen, had just graduated a semester early, and had proven, by my performance at work, that I was trustworthy. And in six months, I'd be a legal gun-toting citizen and full-time employee of Sanderson Bail & Bonds.

But—I bent over and let my forehead bang softly against the wheel—I'd promised Bruce and Casey I'd only go to Covington, and that if my search led to New 2, I'd wait for them to go with me, and not go in alone.

But now, with my mother's letter, I wanted to go right away. I'd waited all these years. I was so close. . . .

The entire night had totally messed with my mind. Ari Selkirk was *not* an indecisive person. I'd had to take care of myself for most of my life, and I'd faced tougher moments than this. Hell, this was downright soft compared to some things.

With that thought, I sat back and slipped the key into the ignition, but before I could turn it, my cell phone rang from inside the backpack.

"Hello."

"How'd it go, kiddo?" It was Bruce.

"Fine. Think I got what I came for. Still have to look through it, though. Hey, tell your brother thanks for his help, okay?" Even though the jerk overcharged me for his investigative services.

"Sure. You still driving back tomorrow? We got two new cases. Could be good for business."

Could be, I thought. Could be even better if I found out who I was and why I was different from every other girl in the world.

"Hey, you still there?"

"Yeah." I paused. "I, uh, have a few more leads to check into and then I'll be back. Should be tomorrow night sometime." I squeezed my eyes closed, feeling like crap that I just didn't come clean and tell him I wanted to go to New 2. But I was too afraid that if I did, he'd say no. Originally, I'd planned to leave Covington in the morning and drive back to Memphis. Now I wasn't sure what to do or why the hell I'd just checked out of the hotel.

Yes, you do. You're going past The Rim. You're going into New 2.

After hanging up with Bruce, I turned the ignition and let the car idle. I needed one day. One day to drive into New 2, visit Charity Hospital, gain access to my birth records, and, hopefully, find my father's name. Although, driving might not be the best option seeing as New 2 was notorious for stolen vehicles. The last thing I wanted, especially after going back on my promise, was to arrive back in Memphis *without* the car.

Maybe the woman at the front desk could point me to a bus station. If there was one nearby, then maybe it was meant to be. If not, then I'd have to wait. But there was nothing wrong with asking, right?

Leaning over, I went to grab my backpack, but movement in the rearview mirror made me freeze.

A dark figure stood behind the car, now totally still. Fear shot lightning fast through my system, and I had the distinct feeling that I'd just dropped straight into a horror film.

Shit. He just stood there, a shadow in the rear window.

Slowly my hand skipped over the backpack and went for the glove compartment. I opened it, feeling for the 9mm Bruce kept there. I was in a company car. There was *always* a backup in each vehicle. Illegal for me to use, but something told me being underage was the least of my worries, and if I could scare him off, then no harm done.

Relief rushed through me as my hand curled around the gun. I straightened, took a deep breath, and forced my mind into training mode. I'd practiced encounters like this a million times—evasion tactics, self-defense, apprehending. . . .

I opened the door and got out of the car.

Tall. Dark blond hair cut short. Black T-shirt. A leather strap diagonally across his chest attached to a round shield behind his back. But what caught my attention and made my heart leap to my throat was the very shiny, very wicked-looking blade in his hand, something in between a dagger and a short sword.

He was solidly built, and when he eyed me up and down and then stared into my eyes, my mother's words echoed in my mind. *RUN!*

My hand flexed on the weapon I held against my thigh as he moved from the trunk of the car to the open space, leaving me trapped between two vehicles and the wall of the hotel. I eased back and slipped between the front of the car and the bushes, and made for the other side. He shadowed my move.

"Look, man, I don't know what your deal is, but maybe you should put the knife down, okay?"

We were on the back side of the hotel, virtually isolated. And unless a car came down the side road next to the lot, I was on my own.

He moved forward, leading with his wide shoulders. I didn't want to shoot the guy, but something told me he could care less about the gun. He started speaking. In a different language. A low, commanding tone spoken with such conviction that I knew whatever he was saying was bad, like *last rites* kind of bad.

"C'mon, don't be stupid." I backed up, stumbling over the curb. "I don't want to shoot you."

He closed the distance between us and was about three feet from me when he spoke in heavily accented English and raised the blade. "By the will of *Athana potniya*, I release you from this life."

Damn it, he's gonna make me do it.

The blade swung down. I fired.

The sound cracked through the night air like a bomb, and the slight kickback vibrated through my body as the bullet thunked into his thigh.

He flinched, paused for a second, and then continued stalking toward me.

My eyes went wide and my mouth went dry. Oh yeah, he was jacked up, high on something. Had to be.

He raised the long dagger again. My pulse pounded loud and slow in my ears. It seemed like that second lasted forever before his arm came down with so much force that it made him grunt. I could barely feel my hand as I leveled the gun and pulled the trigger again. The bullet hit him in the right shoulder. It wouldn't kill him, but it should make him drop the damn mini-sword.

He stopped, arm halfway into his blow, and glanced at the blood blooming outward from his wound. Then his crazy eyes met mine. He grinned.

Oh shit.

He took two steps and swung downward. I caught his arm, hoping the wound and my own strength would be enough to hold him off. His face was inches from mine, close enough for me to see the purpose-filled light in his eyes. Sweat trickled down his left temple. Through clenched teeth, he cursed at me in that odd language. His other fist swung up, but I blocked it with my elbow, steeling myself against the pain, and immediately kneed him in the groin with enough strength to dent the hood of a car. He dropped back and doubled over.

The blade clattered to the ground.

About time.

My senses kicked in. I darted past him, grabbing the blade off the ground without breaking stride, my hair coming undone and falling into my eyes. I made for the side street that led to the front of the hotel, but just as I rounded the corner, he caught up with me. His hand snaked out and hooked my ankle. I shrieked in surprise. My arms pinwheeled. *Oh no.* I braced for impact.

My elbows hit the ground first, a fraction of a second before my forehead cracked hard on the blacktop and sent the gun and blade clattering.

Pain burst in all directions, running along every inch of my skull and blinding me in the process.

Jesus Christ! Everywhere there was searing white light.

My limbs went numb, my pulse thundering too fast, too chaotic. I was on the verge of panic, the kind that would completely destroy my ability to fight if I didn't get my act together. *If you're down, you swing at anything! You do whatever it takes to get back up!* Bruce's voice shouted in my head.

Biting back the panic, I flipped over and kicked out blindly, connecting with something. My hand brushed over the hilt of the blade lying above my head. I grabbed it, sat up, and shoved it in front of me with all my strength, hoping to hell it hit something.

The sword caught. I pushed.

My heartbeat drummed so loud in my ears, I could barely hear. Slowly my vision returned.

The man knelt between my legs, both hands holding a small portion of the blade near the hilt, the rest embedded deep in his chest. His eyes were wide and surprised, as though the idea of failure had never occurred to him.

Time passed. Our gazes stayed locked. At some point, his expression shifted to regret. One hand reached out and lifted a strand of my hair. "So beautiful," he whispered in English. He rubbed it between his bloody finger and thumb. Then he muttered in that same strange language before a cough overtook him. He grimaced, closing his eyelids tightly. My hair trailed through his fingers as he fell back, his body sliding off the blade.

The frogs and crickets continued their night song. The sounds of traffic came back to life. But all those sounds, those sounds that had no idea what had just happened, were muted by my loud, ragged breaths.

My throat grew thick and dry. Tears stung my eyes as I stared at the guy in front of me. He couldn't have been more than twenty-five. Healthy. Good-looking. He could've had a decent life. Met a cute girl. Gotten married. Had babies.

Oh, God. I'd just killed a man—my fingers flexed on the hilt of the blade—with a goddamn miniature sword.

Family time with the Sandersons never covered this.

I swiped the back of one shaking hand over my wet eyes, still gripping the dagger with the other even though my knuckles were white and my fingers were cramping. I couldn't seem to move, couldn't seem to recover from the shock. The shock of being attacked by a stranger. Of fighting for my life. Of killing him … *Get the cell phone. Call 911. Get off your ass, you know what to do.* Yes. I knew what to do. With a few deep breaths to calm my racing heart, I rolled onto one hip to push up, but the man's body suddenly twitched.

I froze, mouth going slack as his body lifted off the ground and hovered for a few seconds before slowly turning to smoke, and then disappearing into some invisible updraft.

Dumbfounded, I sat back down and blinked. My grasp on

the sword went limp, the angle of the blade catching the street-light and making the blood shine.

A sharp laugh escaped my open mouth. "Seriously?" My voice sounded small and weak in the quiet night. I tipped my head back and yelled at the hazy night sky. "Seriously!"

Was this someone's idea of a mind game? Did I fall down the steps at Rocquemore? Bang my forehead too hard on the pavement? *Goddamn it!* Tears blurred my vision as I stared at the blade resting on the ground between my legs.

Blood. Blade.

Whatever had just happened, I knew one thing. It was real. I held the proof of it in my hands. My mother, as screwed up as it sounded, had been right.

Three

AN ENGINE'S DEEP RUMBLE AND THE BLARE OF MUSIC CLICKED into my shocked senses. Bright lights blinded me. The whine of brakes. The smell of rubber burning on asphalt . . . It all reached me too late.

I threw an arm over my face and turned to roll, realizing I was sitting in the side street, in the path of an oncoming vehicle. I'd been caught off guard, distracted by what I'd just done and seen. Blood rushed through my system so fast, my limbs were numb and my head was cloudy.

The truck swerved and came to a rocking halt, the left front bumper so close that I could reach out and touch it. A puff of exhaust breezed over me, the smell turning my stomach. A small figure leaned out of the open driver's side. I removed my arm from over my head as the loud engine vibrated through me like a slow, continuous stream of electricity going for the ground.

"Hey, you okay?" a girl in overalls and a tweed cabbie hat asked.

I tried to respond, but couldn't find my voice.

"You drunk or something?"

"No," I croaked, rolling to my knees and flattening my palms on the asphalt to help push my weak body to its feet. Once I was steady, I brushed my hands on my jeans.

"'Kay. Well, you mind moving? I got mail to dump."

I eyed the girl with her grease-stained overalls, white ribbed tank underneath, flannel shirt, and thin frame. Her brown hair was braided into two plaits, and she had shrewd green eyes, a splattering of freckles over the bridge of her nose, and a smudge of grease on her face. An old UPS logo peeked out from a thin layer of black spray paint on the truck's side. "You're from New 2. One of the mail runners."

"So?"

I swallowed, knowing I was in shock and probably not in the best frame of mind to make a spur-of-the-moment decision, but I knew if I didn't take advantage of the opportunity in front of me, I'd talk myself out of it. One day. All I needed was one day. "I'm looking for a ride into the city."

The girl's left eye squinted, sweeping over me from head to toe, and not shy about it either. "You one of those parrots?"

"Parrots?"

"Yeah, you know . . . paranormal tourists?" She flapped her elbows. "Squawk, squawk!"

"How old are you?"

"Almost thirteen."

My brow lifted. "They let a twelve-year-old deliver the mail?"

The girl rolled her eyes, leaning her forearms on the large steering wheel. "You ain't been to New 2 before, have you?" I shrugged. "Things don't run down there the way they run outside The Rim." Her eyes turned calculating. "You can get in, but it'll cost you."

"How much?"

"Twenty bucks."

"Done. Just give me a sec." I snagged the gun and blade from the ground, then hurried to the car to grab my mother's box. I shoved the sword into my backpack, having to angle it so it'd fit, slid the gun into my waistband, and then locked the car.

"Just gotta dump my bags at the P.O. and then I'm done," the girl said as I got in. Her gaze went briefly to the backpack, but she said nothing about the gun and blade. Instead she stuck out a greasy hand. "I'm Crank."

I took the small hand. "Ari."

Crank shoved the massive stick shift into gear and released

the clutch. The big truck rocked back and forth several times, making me snag the cold metal door handle as it finally lurched into motion.

No one had come out of the hotel when the gunshots were fired. Hadn't they heard? A tingle of unease slid down my back as the sight of the hotel and back parking lot disappeared from view. Either the hotel staff or guests didn't call the cops on purpose, or gunshots in the middle of the night were the norm near The Rim. That might also explain why Crank didn't seem fazed by the weapons I'd brought onboard. But none of those thoughts made me feel any better.

Once Crank drove around to the back of the post office and reversed to a loading dock, she climbed into the rear of the truck, opened the door, and dumped all the mail bags into three large bins. She snagged two bags marked for New 2 from the loading zone and tossed them inside, and then we headed toward Route 190.

Part of the southbound exit was barricaded, but three faded orange barrels had been moved to make a driving space.

We drove for what I guessed was ten miles or so before officially passing over The Rim. There was nothing to mark the occasion except an aging road sign that read: UNITED STATES BORDER. DISASTER AREA AHEAD. PROCEED AT YOUR OWN RISK. And then another sign a few feet down: PROPERTY OF THE NOVEM. PLEASE RESPECT OUR LAND. WELCOME TO NEW ORLEANS.

Besides the bumps and noise of the engine, the ride was long and full of silence—the kind of silence you see, not hear. A silence that stretched across the flat landscapes to the black silhouettes of ruined towns, abandoned fast-food restaurants, gas stations, and vehicles. The road became worse as we progressed, the cracked asphalt riddled with holes and large, random patches of weeds.

"Nothing much out there anymore," Crank said, glancing over at me and following the direction of my gaze. "Most folks live in or around New 2."

"Why would anyone stay?" I asked under my breath. The government had washed its hands of the city and the surrounding land after the devastation, declared it a disaster area, and moved everyone out who wanted to go. The entire city, state, and federal infrastructure in New Orleans collapsed along with its economy. If anyone stayed, it was with the knowledge that America didn't exist there anymore.

Nine of the oldest families in New Orleans had formed an alliance, the Novem, and they bought the ruined city and surrounding counties in a landmark deal that seemed a win-win situation for everyone. The government didn't have to deal with New Orleans. Some of the $8.2 billion the United States earned from the sale went to all the displaced and affected people. And the Novem got something they obviously wanted—a city to call their own.

For a while, the media had been all over the Novem, lured by the intense speculation behind the group's unexplained purchase of a wasteland, and attracted by their wealth and the power that came with owning and running an entire city. There was even a book written about the families and their long history in New Orleans. They gained a kind of celebrity status that grew into something of a legend. The odd characters dotting their family trees only added to the mystery—tales of witches and vampires and voodoo queens.

The Novem never confirmed or denied any rumors. They never gave interviews, never stepped into the spotlight except to make the purchase. And then they retreated into their ruined city, leaving the rest of the country to wonder. It wasn't long before they joined the ranks of Area 51, Roswell, the Loch Ness monster, and all the other conspiracy theories and paranormal speculations out there. The undercover reporters and truth seekers who'd come out of the city later on with grainy photographs and accounts of monsters and murders only added to the speculation. And now, thirteen years later, a large percentage of the country believed New 2 was a sanctuary, a hot spot, for the paranormal.

Crank shrugged, her cheeks jiggling as the truck's tires hit a succession of potholes. "New 2 is home," she answered my quiet question. The springy seat bounced her entire body, drawing my attention to her feet, which rested on wooden blocks attached to the pedals so she could reach. "Some people didn't have anywhere else to go, some were too dang stubborn to leave."

"Which one are you?"

Crank let out a small laugh. "Both, I guess. My dad died in the flood. My uncle hid my brother and mom, like a lot of people did when the troops came through and ordered the city evacuated. I wasn't born until after, though. Why are you going?"

I hugged the box a little tighter. "Trying to find out about my parents. I was born at Charity Hospital a few years before the hurricanes struck."

"No shit, really?"

A small laugh bubbled in my throat. Crank was like a little adult trapped in a prepubescent body. "Really."

"Well, maybe my brother can help you with that. He's pretty good at finding things. You have a place to stay yet?"

Yeah . . . I hadn't actually thought that far ahead when I decided to jump into the mail truck. "No, not yet." All I needed was one day. One day to find the hospital and access my records. I wasn't going to turn back now.

"Good. You can stay with us. Those tourist hotels, the ones in the French Quarter, they are *high* dollar."

The offer was the last thing I expected. But then, I never expected to be driven to New 2 by a twelve-year-old, either. "I don't know. . . ."

"Trust me, we have tons of rooms. Forty bucks will get you one for the night." When I didn't answer right away, she said, "You in?"

"Sure," I said on a sigh, settling in for the ride and rolling my eyes at nothing. "Why not?"

The truck sped through the tattered remains of Mandeville and then passed what used to be the toll area for the Lake Pontchartrain Causeway. There was a dim light inside one of the booths along with a dark, shadowed figure. Crank slowed the truck. The man, at least that's what I guessed by the size of him, waved us through.

I squeezed the oh shit handle tightly as the truck rolled over one side of the double-span bridge; the other side was impassable, missing huge chunks of pavement, leaving only the massive concrete pillars standing, most of which were topped with bird nests.

Crank slid a sideways glance at me, a knowing smile on her lips. She gave the truck a little more gas. "Twenty-four miles to go," she sang under her breath, enjoying my anxiety a little too much. She leaned over, reaching for the radio, her eyes barely seeing over the dashboard. The truck began to veer dangerously close to the guardrail.

My hand tightened around the door handle, the other holding the box tightly. "Um, Crank?"

The radio blared to life and Crank straightened, taking the steering wheel with her and veering to the left side of the road, where a chunk of the guardrail had vanished. Without missing a beat, she settled back into her driving stance and slowly guided the vehicle into the center of the road.

Twenty-four miles of bridge, minus the last hair-raising few, stretched out low and mostly flat over the calm waters of the lake. Twenty-four miles of zydeco music as every one of my stomach muscles grew sore and my fingers began to stiffen around the door handle. By the time we reached land, I felt like I'd done a hundred sit-ups and heard enough zydeco to last a lifetime.

Crank navigated through the suburb of Metairie, which was dark and quiet this time of night, only a few random lights where there should've been thousands, then onto Route 61, which led to Washington Avenue. The street changed names a few times before it intersected with St. Charles Avenue in the Garden District. Crank didn't slow down to check for traffic, just shot out into the intersection, veering left onto the street. Not that it mattered; there wasn't anyone else on the road. There were a few streetlamps working, and I could see the double tracks of the St. Charles Avenue trolley running parallel with the road.

The Garden District had become a semi ghost town, a beautiful lost place where once-manicured gardens surged over their cast-iron fences and spread across the community in a tangle of vines and weeds.

Crank turned down First Street, and it was like we'd gone a hundred years back in time. Despite the chipped paint, rotted boards, busted railings, and cracked, broken, or boarded-up windows, the houses stood like dignified street sentinels surrounded by ancient live oaks draped in the gray, ragged shawls of Spanish moss.

The truck turned onto Coliseum Street and then stopped suddenly, brakes whining, sending me flying forward until my seat belt clicked and stopped me from going through the windshield. I flew back against the seat, heart pounding as Crank shoved the gear into neutral, pressed the parking brake, and turned off the engine.

Leftover vibrations from the rumbling truck continued through me, and my ears felt like they were encased in muffs.

"Home sweet home," Crank said loudly. "Come on."

I hopped out with the box and slung my backpack over my shoulder. My feet hit solid ground. The impulse to drop to my knees and thank God I'd made it out alive went through me, but

I stayed still, taking a second to regain my equilibrium.

"This way," Crank's voice echoed in the darkness.

I stepped onto the broken sidewalk and craned my head back at the tall shadow looming above us. *Wow.*

The house on the corner of First and Coliseum was set in a jungle of trees and overgrown lawn, surrounded by a black iron fence. It was tall and rectangular, two stories high with faded mauve paint, lacy wrought-iron railings and scrollwork along the double porches, and black plantation shutters framing the large windows. A few dim lights shone through the panes, muted by dark curtains, dirt, and grime.

I loved it immediately—beauty shadowed by time and decay, but still standing proud. Yeah, this was my kind of place.

Feeling a little better about my spontaneous decision to come to New 2, I followed Crank through the main gate, which supported a thick, climbing tangle of small, fragrant white flowers—the same kind that wound up the side of the house and twined through the second-floor railing. A black lantern hung suspended from the roof of the second-story porch above us.

"Cool, huh?" Crank said over her shoulder as she opened the front door.

"You live here?"

"Yup. Well, we don't technically *own* it, but no one ever came back to claim it, so now it's ours. There's a bunch of empty ones in the GD—that's what we call the Garden District. The better ones have all been snagged by squatters, but this one ain't half bad. Some rooms are worse than others, but otherwise it's good." She held out her hand. "Twenty for the ride and forty for the room."

"Oh, right." I set my backpack on the porch and fished for my wallet, pulling out three twenties and placing them in Crank's open hand.

We entered into a large hardwood foyer with a wide staircase along one wall, the bottom half of it curving gently toward the front door. The base fanned out like honey spilled from a jar. Hanging on a long chain attached to the second-floor ceiling was a large wrought-iron chandelier, so fine and detailed it looked like it had been spun from some magical metalworking spider. The walls on either side of the foyer had wide openings leading to other rooms.

To the right was a massive dining room with a long, stately table and ten high-backed chairs. There was a faded mural on the ceiling, and burgundy-and-gold wallpaper that was faded and peeling in places. Black sconces burned, minus the two that didn't work, in spaced intervals around the room, and two tall windows were framed with cornices and heavy old burgundy curtains.

"Neat, huh?" Crank stood beside me. "We call it The Crypt 'cause it looks like something from a vampire movie."

"Nice," I murmured.

Some of the floorboards were rotting. I avoided those as we headed for the stairs. The wallpaper in the foyer was missing or peeling in places just like in the dining room, but, like Crank said, it wasn't half bad. In fact, I thought it was just as beautiful on the inside as it was on the outside.

"I'll show you your room first."

Across the foyer from the dining room was the living room. It ran the entire left-side length of the house. Tall ceilings. Two dusty chandeliers. And two fireplaces along the far wall, with gilded mirrors over each mantel. Like the dining room, and probably every other room in the house, the room was framed with serious crown moldings and plasterwork. One of the windows had been boarded up with random pieces of lumber and nails.

"You can stay in the room across from mine," Crank said, already on the stairs. "Oh, and be careful on the sixteenth step."

I counted, making sure to skip number sixteen, and then followed Crank down a wide hallway. She stopped at the first door on the left and then stood back to let me through first. "Here you go."

The bedroom was dark and smelled of damp wood. Crank hit a light switch and a small chandelier glowed above us, hanging from a plaster medallion on the ceiling. The floors were wide, planked hardwood, and there were two tall windows. I entered with careful steps. The floor creaked but held.

"Yours overlooks the side garden. The mattress was growing mold, so we threw that out a long time ago, but I can bring you my old sleeping bag. We've got running water, but I wouldn't drink it if I were you. Just use it for showering and the toilet and you should be fine. Toilet is through that door; every room has its own. The Novem put all their money into fixing the French Quarter first, but eventually we'll get things back to the way they should be out here. I'll tell my brother you're here."

Crank was gone before I could turn around and say thanks, so I stood there in the middle of the old room, taking in the iron bed frame with no mattress, the faded oval rug on the floor, the marble fireplace, and the mantel, which held a bunch of candles, all in different stages of use.

An oil painting of a mother and two children hung over the bed, and on either side of the painting were gilded sconces that didn't seem to be working.

There was a tall bureau in the corner, and a long matching dresser and mirror on the same wall as the fireplace. I walked over, drawn by a human skull snuggled in a bed of colorful Mardi Gras beads, a black top hat on its head. It looked—I gulped—*real*. An old cigar was wedged between its teeth. There were other things on the dresser too—a silver hand mirror and brush, a small jewelry box, and an empty wine bottle with a candle shoved into the neck.

The mirror above the dresser was hazy and cracked in the right-hand corner. The reflection that stared back at me looked quiet and lost. Couldn't argue with that. Never in a million years had I thought I'd go beyond The Rim. Yeah, people did—Mardi Gras revelers, tourists, or scientists wanting to study stories of paranormal occurrences—but otherwise most people just didn't come here.

I stepped to the window and gazed down at the jungle garden. A fat live oak occupied the left-hand corner, but it was buried under vines and long gray tendrils of moss. The lawn had been taken over by a carpet of dead leaves and small purple flowers. A statue of an angel with face and hands lifted to the sky, one wing broken, was partly covered in green lichen. A shiver crawled down my spine. Something was moving under the carpet of leaves.

"I got goodies!" a voice shouted from downstairs. Footsteps and voices echoed beyond the bedroom walls.

Crank's head appeared in the open doorway. "Henri's back."

I set my backpack and the box on the floor near the dresser and then followed Crank down the stairs, but I stopped midway and stared at the group in the foyer, using the iron railing to steady myself.

The one I guessed was Henri held up a large bag of oranges. Crank and two other kids gathered around him. Henri must've been my age or a little older, because he had thin red stubble growing along his jaw and chin. His hair was dark red, uncut, and tied back behind his head. But it was his eyes that made me gasp. Like mine, they weren't normal. The irises bordered on hazel, but they were too light, too yellow, to be normal. Weren't they?

Someone stuck a knife into the bag and a few oranges fell out, bumping the floor. Laughter erupted. Crank and the two others dropped down to corral the loose fruit.

The smallest one hunched over, snatched an orange, and then swung her head around to meet my stare. She was small and slight, almost gaunt, with huge black eyes cradled by dark shadows. Her face was tiny, oval, and white, save for the faint pink of her lips. Her shaggy black bob curled under her chin. Resting against her chest, and held there by a small string around her neck, was a gold Mardi Gras mask.

The girl grinned slowly, revealing a small row of white teeth and two very distinct, very tiny . . . fangs.

My pulse leaped. I jerked my gaze off the little girl.

Get a grip, Ari.

The group below me became quiet. All staring. At me. My heart pounded. Slowly my hand released the railing and I turned, going woodenly back up the stairs.

What the hell was I doing here?

New 2 was a weird-ass place. I knew that going in, but . . .

It wasn't until I was inside the room, walking toward my things, that I heard them talking in whispers, followed a moment later by their footsteps on the stairs.

"Crank said you're looking for information," Henri said, leaning against the door frame, arms crossed over his chest.

I picked up my backpack. "Not anymore."

He entered the room, shaking his head. "What, you were expecting a five-star hotel? A bunch of teens with cell phones and iPods and the latest clothes from Abercrombie and Fitch?"

I bit my tongue rather than tell him that iPods were ancient history and Abercrombie & Fitch went out of business ages ago. I bent down for the box.

"What's with the gun?"

Shit. I straightened, realizing the 9mm was sticking out of my waistband for the entire world to see. "It's legal." But I wasn't.

"That's not what I meant."

I really didn't want to get into a play-by-play of what I was doing here and why I was armed. Actually, it was becoming pretty obvious I'd made a huge mistake.

Henri blocked my path. Beyond his shoulder Crank and the others stood in the doorway, eyes wide and listening. I backed up and glared at Henri. "Do you mind?"

After a short, tense silence, he threw up his hands and moved aside. "Fine, be my guest. I don't know how you're going to get back to The Rim without a ride. Good luck finding a taxi or a Greyhound bus." The others laughed.

I gave him a twisted smile. "Thanks." And then stormed around him as the other three scattered from the exit. I was being dramatic and stupid, I knew, but the little girl's teeth . . . Henri's eyes . . . It hit too close to home, made me think of my own weirdness, and it made me want to run like I always did.

My boots slapped hard against each step as I jogged down the stairs, careful to miss the broken one, and wondered why the hell I'd thought this was a good idea. All I wanted was to find out about my mother, and by coming to New 2 and accessing the hospital records, maybe my father's name. That was all, just a name. An actual family history would be great, but I was smart enough to know that was like reaching for the stars.

And I *should* have been smart enough to avoid New 2 and wait, like I'd promised, until Bruce and Casey could go with me. But then, I didn't expect to get that freaky-ass letter from my mother or be attacked by a foreign, disappearing weirdo, either.

I was halfway across the foyer when the front door opened and another guy stepped through.

His head was down, a lock of raven hair shielding his face. One hand held the strap to an old backpack as the other one pushed the door closed behind him. Tall. Six-one, maybe. He had on ratty jeans, black boots, and an old Iron Maiden T-shirt faded to a soft gray. Around his left wrist was a dark leather bracelet with a silver inlaid band.

I froze. Like a total moron.

His head came up, and I was met with the most startling gray eyes I'd ever seen. In my peripheral vision, I saw his backpack slowly slide out of his hand and hit the floor.

My mouth went paper dry, too dry to swallow. Heat engulfed my face and the small of my back. His black eyebrows were drawn into a scowl that gave him a slightly sinister appearance, but they were in definite contrast to the soulful eyes framed with thick, inky black lashes. He had a nice face, one that I'd bet could go from poet to tough guy depending on his mood. His lips were naturally darker than most, and they tightened as his eyes continued to narrow. His jaw flexed. I stepped back, feeling odd, like he could see inside of me, like he knew what I was.

"They're already looking for you, you know."

Four

A LUMP ROSE IN MY THROAT, AND I IMMEDIATELY THOUGHT OF the blade-wielding maniac. I bit the inside of my cheek so hard the skin split, releasing warm, iron-rich blood onto my tongue. "Who's looking for me?"

"The Novem."

"Yeah," I said, putting two and two together, "they already tried to kill me once. I won't let them get that close a second time."

His brows drew together. "The Novem doesn't want to kill you."

Crank came around me and jumped onto the long table against the wall, sitting on it and swinging her feet. "He's right, you know."

I shook my head, not understanding. "How would you know?"

"'Cause Sebastian's my brother, and he knows everything that happens in New 2. It's his *job* to know." I cocked an eyebrow at him, waiting for him to at least agree, but he stayed silent. "Bas works for the Novem. They pay him to run messages, get info, that sort of thing." Crank twisted her cabbie hat backward. "So who's really after you, Ari? Does it have anything to do with that bloody sword in your backpack?"

I let my eyelids close slowly and then counted to five. I had killed a man. Seen him disappear. There was a tiny Goth girl with *fangs*. And now the Novem might or might not be after me. I was guessing "might," no matter what Crank said.

How the hell did I get into this mess? No, this wasn't *my* mess, this was my mother's. And I wasn't so sure I wanted to know the truth anymore. I pulled my cell phone from the holder on my waist. Bruce would come get me. He'd be mad as hell, but he'd come.

"Cell phones don't work in New 2," Henri said from behind me.

I glanced at the display. No signal. "Fine. Is there a phone or a pay phone somewhere I can use?"

"Newbies," a boy around Crank's age muttered, sitting on one of the steps to peel his orange. He was so odd-looking that he distracted me for a second. Light brown skin. Green eyes.

And a short dark blond Afro. Even his eyebrows were blond.

"Unless you got money or connections, no phones, no Internet. Nothing but running water, electricity, and mail runners," Henri said. "Welcome to New 2."

"Ari was born at Charity Hospital. She wants to find her records. You can help with that, can't you, Bas?" Crank asked her brother.

Sebastian picked his backpack up, avoiding my eyes. "No. She should go back home." He walked up the stairs.

Crank sputtered, and no one else said a word. The only sound was Sebastian's unhurried footsteps on the stairs. I glanced from the front door to the stairs and then let out a groan, not believing I was about to run after Mr. Warm & Welcoming.

I jogged up the steps, catching up to Sebastian on the landing. "Hey, hold on a sec." He stopped, turning partway. "Look, if you know something . . . why these people are after me . . ."

At five-eight, I wasn't that much shorter than Sebastian, but I felt small under his storm-cloud gaze. The guy gave nothing away. He tossed a quick glance to the others, who had gathered halfway up the stairs. His jaw clenched and his eyes went hard. He bent forward and kept his voice low. "The Novem got a call a few hours ago with your description and name . . . the word went out to all the runners and people who work for the Novem— which is basically everyone in this city—to look for you."

Dr. Giroux. He must've called. But why? "And you work for them."

"They just want to see you. No one said anything about hurting you, so I don't know shit about that whole sword thing Crank is talking about. And yeah, I work for them. Doesn't mean I always listen."

He marched down the hall and disappeared into a room at the end.

A wave of exhaustion settled over me. My shoulders slumped. I could feel the others' eyes on me from below, and more than anything I just wanted to be left alone so I could regroup and think straight, to digest everything that had happened so far. My hasty decision or desire—whatever you wanted to call it—to bolt wouldn't do me any good. It was dark. I needed a place to stay. I'd already paid. And, I sighed, I guessed this was it.

I went back into the bedroom, snagged the box, and sat on the rug in front of the fireplace. But the shuffle of footsteps in the hall made it clear I wouldn't be getting privacy anytime soon.

Crank, the odd-looking boy, and tiny fang girl—who was now *wearing* the gold Mardi Gras mask—filed into the room. They sat on the rug, making a circle. The boy leaned toward the fireplace and snapped his fingers over the wood. It burst into flames.

He held his hands over the fire, warming them before turning back to the others. "No big deal. Just a trick," he said at my open mouth. "What's in the box?"

Yeah, just a freaking trick. It was easier to believe that than the alternative. "Stuff about my mother."

A drum echoed from somewhere down the hall. Then another and another, until a rhythm took hold. The walls and the floor vibrated. The tempo picked up, fast, furious, and seriously good, seeping into my skin and bones, finding its way to my heart and beating in time.

"That's Sebastian," Crank said. "He plays when he's in a mood."

I didn't have to ask what that meant. I knew moods as well as the next person. In the background, very faintly, I heard music and vocals, and realized that he must be playing in time to the radio or a CD. Whatever it was, it was something you could dance to, or lie down on the floor, close your eyes, and weep to.

As the flames in the fireplace grew, shadows danced on the walls and over the skull, which seemed to grin at me as though it knew something I didn't. Firelight glinted off the colorful beads and the black satin of the top hat. *It needs a name,* I thought, wondering which was creepier, the skull or the little girl who stared at me through the gold mask with those luminous black eyes.

"This is Dub," Crank said, motioning to the boy. "And this is Violet. She doesn't talk much."

Violet still cradled her orange in both hands, occasionally bringing it up to her tiny nose to smell it, but her round eyes were fixed on me. She looked like some strange Mardi Gras Goth doll. And for some reason, I found myself warming to the odd little kid. She couldn't have been more than ten years old.

"I think she likes your tattoo," Dub said, tapping his fingers on his khakis. "Are you a *doué* too?"

"A what?"

"*Doué.* That's the Novem's nice word for freaks. Weirdos. You know . . . *us*," he explained in a fast breath. Everything about Dub was nervous energy. Some part of his body constantly moved. "Violet's got freaky teeth. Henri's got weird eyes. I got tricks. Crank's got—"

"Nothing," she cut in, disappointed. "I'm the normal one."

"Yeah, but no one else can make things work like you do," Dub said. "And"—he put one hand over his heart and the other straight out like he was about to serenade her—"since you fixed the fridge, you *rule* this house of freaks."

Crank's head dipped, and she rolled her eyes, but I could see she was pleased with the compliment. "And your brother, Sebastian," I asked. "Is he normal too?" *Besides being a jerk and a kick-ass drummer.*

"Sebastian doesn't like to talk about it. But he reads people, you know? He feels what they feel. Sometimes too much."

The drums still banged, but not so demanding as before, not so fast. Now it was a steady, even rhythm full of emotion. There was no other way to describe it. It wasn't just a beat echoing down the hall, it was something more.

"So what about you?" Dub asked again more quietly. "You look weird and everything."

"Gee, thanks."

"Well, you got that tattoo on your face, your hair is white, and your eyes are a little freaky." He shrugged. "You *could* be a *doué* is all I'm sayin'."

"Maybe she doesn't like to talk about it either," Crank said, giving me a small smile. I returned the smile and then looked down at my hands. It was the truth; I didn't like to talk about it. I never had. And suddenly sharing wasn't something I'd ever do.

"Holy smokes," Dub said. I looked back up to see him pulling the blade from my backpack. "It's got blood on it and everything!"

"Give me that!" I lunged onto my knees, snatching the hilt, and then my backpack, out of his hand.

"Sheesh. *Sorry*." He sat back down, acting as if I'd made a big deal out of something small. But it wasn't small. He had no business going into my things. None at all.

I shoved the short sword into the backpack, hoping the blood was dried by now and hadn't gotten all over my clothes. *Smart one, Ari.* Should've thought about that before I put the thing in there to begin with. "Look, just stay out of my things, okay? I'll be out of your hair by morning."

"I can try to talk to Bas again," Crank said. "I'm sure he'll help you at the hospital, and—"

"No offense, Crank, but I don't want his help."

Crank nudged Dub on the arm, and they stood. Violet stayed motionless, so Crank reached down and tugged on her arm. "Come on, Vi."

The dark little girl hissed at Crank, but got up and left with the others.

After Crank brought me the sleeping bag, I waited until silence descended beyond my bedroom door, a silence broken only by the natural creaks and moans of the house.

I took two tall candles from the mantel and lit them with the red-hot coals in the fireplace, setting them on the floor in front of me. Finally, I was alone. No interruptions. No kids. No drums. Nothing to distract me. Though, honestly, it had taken me this long just to work up the nerve to see whatever else was in the box.

With a deep breath, I opened the two small jewelry boxes

first. In one was a silver ring with a Greek inscription running along its length. It was polished and beautiful and simple. I placed it on my right hand, fourth finger. It fit perfectly. The next box held a worn medallion, so worn that it was hard to make out the image on the front or the words that went around the edge. It might've been a sun, I couldn't tell for sure. I put the medallion back in the box and then picked up a newspaper clipping about a woman beheaded in Chicago, leaving a small daughter, Eleni, behind with no family. My heart gave a hard bang. *Holy shit.* Eleni was my mother's name, so this woman could be my grandmother.

The next was a faded letter written to my mother.

Dear Eleni,

If you are reading this then I have been unsuccessful, like so many others before me. I have failed you.

As you grow and reach womanhood, you will understand that you are different. All of us have been this way. No woman in our family as far back as I've uncovered has lived beyond her twenty-first birthday. We have all left behind a daughter. It seems fate has chosen our path for us, and it is always the same.

You will be no different. Unless you can find a way to stop this curse. My mother killed herself when I was a baby. She left me nothing, but I've learned that her mother, and her mother before her, also died in the same way.

And soon I will go too. I feel it in my bones, under my skin. My time is coming. I have tried, have seen so many cultists, quacks, and priests, but this curse is still with me as it will be with you. But I refuse to give in to the madness. I refuse. I will not give in to this urge to end things. Perhaps that alone will break the curse.

Find the cure, Eleni. Stop this madness inside of us. I wish we had more time together. . . .

I will always be with you,

Mother

Tears stung my eyes, and a lump swelled my throat. I folded the letter carefully and slid it back into its envelope. I didn't want to believe it, but inside I knew. The words were true. Fate had had its way with all of them, and now it was my turn. A warm drop fell on my cheek, and I brushed it away.

Screw this.

I wasn't about to die *or* get pregnant in the next three and a half years. This thing, this curse or whatever it was, would end with me. The beheading of my grandmother meant that something came for her, killed her, when she refused to give in to the madness and kill herself. And something came for me in the parking lot of the hotel—a bit shy of my twenty-first birthday, sure, but definitely looking to end me.

I rubbed both hands down my face.

I didn't have enough information. The only things I knew for sure was that I was different—I'd known that all my life—some *thing* had tried to kill me, and the women in my family were cursed, all of them dead at twenty-one.

Twenty-one. Twenty-fucking-one.

I rested my chin on the tepee of my fingers, trying to find some calm and direction amid the chaos that had become my life in one night. I had killed the thing that came for me. Maybe that alone had broken the curse.

Weak theory.

But . . . I was here now. In New 2. The only logical thing to do was to find out more about my mother, my father, and why the Novem wanted to see me. Or hurt me.

One day. I'd give it one day.

{} {} {}

I woke to bruised elbows, an achy forehead, and a stiff back. And, if the red behind my eyelids was any clue, a shaft of sunlight spilling through the window. I squeezed my lids closed as a shadow blocked the light. The floorboards creaked. I opened my eyes.

Every muscle froze. I was looking straight into the blue eyes of a small white alligator.

"Pascal, this is Ari," a tiny feminine voice whispered.

It was Violet—on her knees, leaning over the sleeping bag, a burgundy, jewel-encrusted mask pushed atop her head—holding a small white alligator directly in front of my face. All it had to do was snap and my nose would be history.

I held my breath, afraid to breathe on its milky skin.

Finally Violet sat back on her heels and turned the alligator to kiss its nose. "Good, Pascal," she whispered, and set him on the floor, pulling the half-mask down over her face. The corners swept up into points adorned with two small feathers.

Pascal waddled away and out the door.

Releasing my breath, I sat up, unsure of what to say to the peculiar girl, who had returned to her staring. Her tiny white hands were laid flat on her knees, and the black dress she wore looked like it had once been a woman's cocktail dress. She had on tights underneath, or they might've been knee-high socks meant for an adult, but whatever they were, they disappeared under the hem of the dress. Her shoes were boy's penny loafers and a size too big.

"Was that your alligator?" I checked the door to make sure Pascal hadn't decided to come back in.

"He is no one's." Violet cocked her head. "He likes your hair. It's like his skin."

Without thinking, I reached up and shoved a loose strand behind my ear, forgetting that I'd unwound it before bed. What I wanted to do was gather it up and shove it behind my shoulders, but for some reason I didn't want Violet to think the hair meant anything, so I left it hanging long and loose, veiling the sides of my face, the ends resting in my lap.

"He likes my teeth. They're like his teeth," Violet said, her large eyes blinking through the holes of the mask.

I stayed still, almost frozen. "Why are your teeth like his, Violet?" I braced myself, hoping the question wouldn't set her off and make her go all fang-girl on me.

"To eat things, of course." Her head cocked. "You are different." Then she stood and walked out with silent steps despite the heavy black shoes.

I watched her disappear from view, a little confused and thrown by how much she fascinated me. But it was more than the masks, and her sharp teeth. Violet made me feel softer inside, like some kind of weird big sister/mothering instinct was being awakened. I guessed it was the same feeling Casey and Bruce had when they first met me—just an unexplainable connection or need to care. I shook my head. Didn't matter, though. I'd be gone tonight.

I went to drag my gaze away from the door when Sebastian passed by, his head turning. It was clear by the falter in his step that he didn't expect to see me sitting there.

My stomach flipped. Heat stung my cheeks. His gray eyes drew me in like two fascinating pools of liquid mercury. *Yeah, and mercury is poison, you big dummy.*

But he wasn't looking at me, I realized; he was looking at my hair. Just like everyone else.

It seemed like forever, but in reality, it was only a second or two before his gaze dropped and his footsteps continued on.

I blinked out of my haze, quickly gathered my hair, and began twisting it as I got to my feet and headed after him. "Sebastian!"

He stopped halfway down the stairs, body language screaming reluctance as I approached, tying my hair into a knot and trying to ignore the fact that the guy made me extremely self-conscious.

Two steps above him, I dropped my arms to my sides. "Look, I know you don't want me here, but . . . the Novem, do you really believe they're not out to hurt me?"

One corner of his mouth almost lifted into what might've been a smile. Or a grimace. "Yes, I do," he answered.

I bit my lip, making a quick decision. "If you help me find the information I'm after, I'll go with you, willingly, to see the Nov—"

The front door flew open, slamming against the wall, the knob sinking through the drywall.

Violet appeared, stopping just inside the parlor with Pascal tucked under her arm, as three young men entered the house.

They were all similar in age—late teens, early twenties. The guy in the middle tossed a glance at Violet, shaking his head. "Welcome to The House of Misfits."

His friends laughed as he lifted his eyes to the stairs. "Adding another one to the ranks?" His attention shifted from Sebastian to me. "Darlin', you're better off in the swamp than with these losers."

"What do you want, Ray?" Sebastian's hand gripped the railing so hard his knuckles turned white.

I took another step down as Dub shuffled from the dining room with an orange, starting to peel it, when Ray snatched it out of his hand.

"Hey!"

Ray threw it on the ground. "What's up, Dub? You half-breed little shit."

"Fuck you, Ray*mond*."

Ray reached for Dub.

It seemed like the next few seconds happened in slow motion.

Violet put Pascal on the ground, pulled her mask over her face as though preparing for battle, and then launched her small body at Ray. She was on him like an octopus, arms and legs wrapped around his middle. Her sharp teeth sank into his bicep. He shrieked, trying to pull her off. He succeeded in getting space between them, but Violet's legs and hands clung tight. He cursed in French and yanked again at her, this time flinging her small body across the room. She hit the floor and slid down the smooth hardwood hall.

Something in me snapped.

I flew around Sebastian and down the stairs as Dub and Crank ran to Violet. Violet stood up on her own, swiped the blood from her mouth and chin, and then darted out the back of the house and into the garden. I just caught a glimpse of her diving under the dead leaves before I turned back to Ray.

Adrenaline thrummed through my veins, fueled by fury. Nothing got me going like seeing a kid being hurt—I knew first-hand what that was like. "Why don't you try that on me?" Better yet, I slugged him in the jaw.

The pain that shot through my knucklebones and up my hand felt good. And when his friends came to his aid, I welcomed the fight.

Bring it on, you assholes.

As the first guy reached out, I spun on my heel and grabbed his arm over my shoulder, flipping him onto the floor. As soon as he was down, the other one's breath fanned the back of my neck. My gaze met Sebastian's. His eyes were smiling at me, challenging me, seeing what I could do. I cocked a grin as the second guy grabbed me around the waist. I threw back my head, bracing for the crack as my skull collided with his face. He grunted. It hurt him way more than it did me. I spun and kicked him in the gut. He went down next to his friend.

I took a step back and surveyed my handiwork, heart racing.

Dub whistled from somewhere behind me. But my attention was fixed on Ray. He was the only one *not* on the floor and therefore still a threat.

"You fucking bitch!" he snarled, one hand over his bloody shoulder and the other rubbing his jaw. His face was a shade paler than when he'd first arrived.

I smirked and flipped him the bird. Red blushed through his skin, and his lips drew back slightly as though he was about to bare his teeth.

Sebastian appeared beside me. "She's mine," he said in a calm voice. "I found her first."

"Yeah, and you just got to be the golden boy, don't you, Lamarliere?" He spit on the floor as his friends finally managed to stand. "Oh, and you'd better get her there soon. Otherwise *Grandmère* will start wondering."

After they were gone, Dub wrenched the door handle from the drywall so the door would close, as I whirled on Sebastian. "I'm *yours*? What the hell was that?"

"Ray works for the Novem too. He's just trying to find you first. Someone must have seen you come in with Jenna."

"Jenna?"

"Crank." He paused. Four seconds went by. "I'll help you find the records." And then he walked toward the back door.

All righty, then.

Drawing in a deep breath—I was going to need it dealing with Mr. Personality—I followed him through a set of massive French doors to the backyard garden. Dub and Crank were standing on a moss-covered stone patio, staring at a lump in the leaves. Despite the winter season, humidity had settled over the district, making the garden more like a jungle, a damp place that reeked of earth, decaying leaves, and those pungent white flowers that crawled up the house.

"Vi, he's gone. And you missed Ari's *awesome* smack-down." Dub reinforced his words with a few air punches and an imaginary body slam. "C'mon, Vivi. You stood up for me. Come on out so I can say thanks in person."

Two black eyes blinked beneath the leaves. I slid closer to

Sebastian as Crank talked to Violet. "What's her deal, anyway? What's with the baby vampire teeth?"

"She's not a vamp," he said with a quiet laugh. "Dub found her out in the swamp last year. She was living alone in a trapper's houseboat. He fed her for three months before she came back with him. She comes and goes as she pleases, takes to weird things like the masks and fruit. Never eats it, though."

My eyebrow lifted, and I rocked back on my heels. "So you actually *do* speak more than one sentence at a time."

He glanced over and frowned. "Come on, we better go. Violet will come out when she's ready."

Five

"IT'S NICE HERE," I SAID, LOST IN THE SCENERY OF THE GARDEN District as I walked with Sebastian to St. Charles Avenue. His only response was a grunt. I hadn't meant to give voice to my thoughts, to share anything with him. It was pretty obvious he didn't have any interest in conversation.

Not that I minded; it wasn't like I was known for my social skills anyway.

So I settled into a nice rhythm next to my guide, keeping my thoughts to myself, minding the cracks in the pavement and the tree limbs that hung low over fences, pulled down by moss or heavy vines.

If someone could've crawled inside my soul and then created a town to fit me best, it would've looked just like the GD. There was a sense of belonging here that I'd never felt anywhere else before. It could've been because I was born here, and I knew my mother had lived here, but somehow it was more than that. It was in the emotion of the place, the air of abandonment, the slight decay on everything, the wildness of the plants and trees, the haunted appearance that clung to the grand old houses, and the dark parts where light never reached—deep in the lost gardens, behind vacant lots, and beyond boarded-up windows. It was even in the misfits that made this place home. In Violet, Dub, Henri, and Crank. And, I glanced over, in Sebastian with his black hair, brooding eyes, and dark red lips. It was the freedom of being in a place that didn't give a shit what you were, because it was different too.

It wasn't entirely neglected, though. We passed a house with a bunch of twentysomething artist types. A guy on the porch played a twelve-string guitar, fingers flying in a romantic Spanish tune as a woman in a turban painted a picture on a canvas. Voices and the sound of hammers on wood flowed from the open windows. Another person lay in an old hammock hung between columns, a joint wedged in the V of his slack fingers.

The guitar guy looked up and dipped his head at Sebastian.

A few more houses and we crossed St. Charles Avenue to wait for the trolley.

"Charity Hospital, right?"

"Yeah. Do you think we'll have trouble accessing my records?"

Sebastian shrugged, dragging his fingers through his hair and leaving it all wild and rumpled. "Shouldn't be too hard."

"Do you know any Selkirks living in New 2?"

The streetcar rolled toward us as Sebastian shook his head and then fished in his pocket for money. "Costs a dollar twenty-five."

"Oh . . . crap." I dropped my backpack on the ground and unzipped the front pocket to pull out two dollars as the trolley came to a stop. Sebastian was already halfway up the steps. I hurried on, paid my fare, and then sat on the wooden bench directly across the aisle from him.

We rode in silence, the only two on the trolley, until Sebastian slid over into my seat, surprising me. I scooted toward the window. "So," he began in a low voice, keeping his eye on the streetcar operator, "you want to tell me about the guy who tried to kill you?"

Our shoulders touched, and I tried not to breathe in too deeply because he smelled really freaking good. "Not really." I stared out the window.

"You think he lived in New 2?"

I frowned. "I don't know what to think. The guy acted like he lived on a different planet." I turned away again and muttered, "A different country, at least. I shot him twice, and he barely flinched." The images of last night came back to me. "Weird thing about it ... my mother *knew*. She died a long time ago, but she knew someone would come after me. She left me this letter, and then like magic there he was."

"And you killed him," he said solemnly, eyes sad for me, for what I'd had to do.

"With his blade, yeah, I killed him. I think." I thought of how my attacker had vanished. I wasn't sure what had really happened to the guy. Maybe he had died, or maybe he'd disappeared to lick his wounds. But I wasn't about to tell Sebastian that part of the story. Hell, I wasn't even sure why I'd told him as much as I had.

The trolley swayed slightly, pushing me toward Sebastian, my nose inches from his. My mouth went dry. Warmth blossomed in my belly. A sense of safety filled me, but it wasn't a calming feeling. It was tense and exciting all rolled into one. His eyes roamed my face and then parked on my lips. A muscle ticked in his jaw. I stopped breathing.

And then the trolley stopped and I caught myself before my ass slipped off the smooth wooden bench.

"Canal Street!" the trolley operator called.

Sebastian was already up and walking away.

Quickly I straightened up, giving myself a hard mental shake. I was here for a reason, not to make goo-goo eyes at some guy just because he was a seriously dark soul who just happened to be killer cute and could play the drums like nobody's business. If he had weird-ass abilities like me, I was in serious trouble.

"We need one more streetcar. The one on Canal Street. That will take us close to the hospital. Then we'll walk the rest of the way. It won't be far," he said as I hopped off.

After we got on the Canal Street trolley, we rode the rest of the way in silence, which was fine by me. My attention was stuck on the ruins of the business district and Midtown. All those high-rises and buildings, in shambles or gutted—everything looking like a casualty of an apocalypse. It was clear the Novem hadn't even touched those places.

Once we were off the trolley, we hiked three blocks or so to Charity Hospital. Sebastian darted across the street, but I stood still, taking in the large building. This was where my mother had given birth to me. My pulse picked up. Did my father come for the birth? Did he walk through that front door with flowers? Balloons? A big ole white teddy bear?

"Ari!" Sebastian stood on the sidewalk, holding up his hands in a *What's going on?* gesture.

Snap out of it. I mimicked the gesture with probably more sarcasm than he deserved, and then jogged over, ignoring his questioning look and heading to the main entrance.

He caught up to me at the doors. "You should wait here."

A small laugh escaped my lips as the doors slid open. "You've got a lot to learn about me. I don't wait in the wings." I led the way inside. I could hear him already. *I don't want to learn about you. I'd rather be sitting in the corner scowling at anyone who dares to pass by.*

We walked past the lobby and down the main hall.

"The records will be in the computers."

"I thought you guys didn't have—"

"We have computers. Paper doesn't exactly last long in this climate. After the Novem bought New 2, they had everything that was left on paper transferred to computer."

We stopped at the elevator. Sebastian hit the down button, and the doors slid open immediately. We entered. "So, what's the plan? Just waltz into the records room and take what we want?"

"Yes."

"Oh wow. That's impressive." I rolled my eyes. The elevator went down a level and then dinged. I strode off before the door was completely open.

A cold silence greeted me. Our footsteps echoed in the empty space. I tried not to think about what was usually kept down in the basement level of most hospitals, but that didn't stop chills from zinging up my spine.

Sebastian veered left and opened a door labeled RECORDS. Just swept right in like he owned the place. Suspicion pooled in my gut. This was way too easy.

There were four desks, two empty, the other two occupied by women, who glanced up from their monitors.

It took at least three seconds for it to dawn on them that we weren't hospital staff, but teens. Odd ones, dressed in denim and black, and, no doubt, up to no good.

Which, actually, was the truth. The thought made me grin.

The older one stood and went to open her mouth.

Sebastian was suddenly there in front of her, so fast I didn't see him move. He reached out, cupping her cheek in his palm. She lifted her chin, entranced, stuck on his gaze. He bent down, his lips brushing her ear as he whispered. Her eyelids fluttered.

The other woman seated at her desk couldn't move, transfixed by the sight of Sebastian and her coworker locked in an intimate embrace where no one else seemed to matter. His hand slid off the woman's cheek. She sank back down to her chair, eyes wide, unseeing, lost in some fantasy of her own mind. Sebastian turned to the other woman. My heart raced as though I was witnessing something private and intimate. Something not for me. But I was rooted to the spot. I couldn't move or leave or look away, even though I wanted to.

The younger woman surged to her feet as Sebastian came forward. He was taller than her by a head and so calm, so focused. When he reached out and trailed a finger down her jaw, she moaned as though she'd been dreaming of being touched like that her whole life. He whispered to her as well, and soon she was sitting in la-la land just like her coworker.

Sebastian faced me. My lips parted. Heat had spread in a slow, steady wave from the center of my torso outward. It felt claustrophobic, stifling. I cleared my throat. "Neat trick. What are you, some kind of hypnotist or something?"

His eyes held mine a second longer than necessary, and the warmth began to rise again. But then he rolled the younger woman away from the computer, faced her monitor, and began typing.

"Mother's name?"

I went to the desk. "Eleni Selkirk."

"Your date of birth?"

"June twenty-first, 2009."

"Any birthmarks, defects? Caesarean or natural delivery?"

Yeah, one gigantic defect, I wanted to say. Instead I said, "None. And I don't know about the other."

He tapped the keyboard a few more times and then stood aside. "There it is. Selkirk baby. Female. Father unlisted."

I scanned the monitor, already in denial. It couldn't be. He *had* to be listed. But as I searched, there was nothing of use in the report, nothing I didn't already know. "Nothing."

Sebastian leaned down and selected the billing tab. "Let's see who paid the bill. It'll have insurance info and who else was on the card, if any."

Okay, I should've thought of that, and having been given a second, I probably would have. The billing info loaded onto the screen. Insurance info. No one on the card except for Eleni. But the co-pay: "Josephine Arnaud. Who the hell is that?"

Sebastian straightened. His jaw tightened and his expression went grim. He dragged his fingers through his hair and then fixed me with a seriously pissed-off look. "Josephine Arnaud is my grandmother."

The women started to move in their chairs, coming out of whatever trance Sebastian had put them in. He clicked back to the main screen, grabbed my arm, and propelled me out the door. "Come on, we'll talk on the way."

I was still trying to recover from the shock of what he'd said, and here he was shoving me toward the door before I could get my bearings. "Wait, hold on, on the way where?" We were through the door and out into the hallway. I jerked my arm from him. "Goddamn it, Sebastian! What the hell is going on?"

I knew I was being too loud, but at that point I didn't give a crap who heard me. Sebastian ushered me into the nearest room. The morgue.

I stepped back from the door. "Well?"

"The Novem is made up of nine families—"

"Yeah, look, I don't need a goddamn history lesson, all right? I know all about the nine families. Everybody does."

Sebastian shook his head, annoyance flashing in his gray eyes. "Outsiders think they know everything. Josephine, my grandmother, is head of the Arnaud family. The Arnaud family is one of the nine who bought New Orleans thirteen years ago."

A short laugh burst through my mouth. But he wasn't laughing. He was deadly serious. "*Your* family. Your family owns part of New 2." I paced in a small circle, giving another disbelieving laugh. "And your *granny* knew my mother and paid her doctor bills. This is unbelievable." I turned my back on him and placed my hands on my hips. Anger coursed through my veins as my eyes slowly took in the sterile room—the exam table, the two carts with two bodies under blue cotton tarps set against a wall of small square doors that probably held more bodies. . . .

Seriously unbelievable. I spun back round, forcing myself to remain there. Putting your back to two dead bodies was definitely not something that felt anywhere near comforting.

I shook my head and cursed softly, not understanding any of it. My mother's warning, the attack, the disappearing dead guy. The curse that now apparently extended to me, and now this—a head of the Novem actually paying my mother's medical bills. Did they know about me, then? Is that why they wanted to see me? Had they been looking for me this whole time?

"So, what now? Go have a talk with dear old Grams? Ask

her why she tried to have me *killed*?" I ran my hands down my face, shaking my head and denying this was all even happening.

"Yeah, that was the plan. I think we should go talk to her."

"Sure you do. That's what you do, right? Do what they say." I backed away, the rush of paranoia fueling my fear like lighter fluid on hot coals. "Thanks, but no thanks. I think this is where we part ways."

I moved to the other side of the exam table, putting some distance between me and Sebastian. My hands curled around the cold edges, ready to shove it at him if he so much as twitched the wrong way.

One corner of his mouth lifted up slightly into what might've been a sad smile. "That would hardly stop me if I wanted to hurt you."

I cast a quick glance over my shoulder, looking for another way out of the room. But there was none. Sebastian stood in front of the only exit. He regarded me patiently, like a parent waiting for a child to get over a fit, and it made me want to slap the look off his face.

"Ari," he said finally, "Josephine Arnaud is a bitch and a manipulator, but she's not a killer. The Novem doesn't employ sword-wielding foreigners, and I'll stake my life on that. If she knew your mother, then she probably has every answer you've ever wanted. I won't let her or anyone else hurt you."

"You don't even know me! You don't even *want* to know me, so why the hell are you going to protect me?"

He was quiet for a long moment, completely unreadable. His eyes darkened to steel gray. The muscle in his jaw ticked a few times before he said, "We're the same. I know what it's like—"

"Oh, please. You don't *know*, okay? You don't know anything. You have no idea what—"

"—it's like to be different? A freak among freaks? Try me. You're in New 2, Ari. Half the kids around here don't even go to school. They have jobs. *Jobs*. The other half are Novem and more fucked up than you could ever imagine."

So much of me wanted to meet his challenge, to tell him exactly how bizarre I really was, but I bit my tongue. It wasn't worth it. And it wasn't like he was going around telling me all about his weird-ass hypnotic abilities anyway. Why should I share mine?

"Whatever," he finally said, and opened the door. "Do what you want."

Screw him. He could leave if he wanted to. I was better off on my own. I'd *always* been better off on my own. This was New 2, *the* place for all things supernatural. If there was any way to learn more about my curse, it was here. I didn't need Sebastian. *Yeah, and your own mother lived here, yet she'd failed to lift the curse.* I chewed softly on the inside of my cheek. It was still raw from where I'd bitten it before.

I let out a frustrated sigh as that realization sank in. "How much do you know about curses?"

Sebastian stilled. I knew what he was thinking, that he should just leave and be rid of me and my bad attitude, and maybe it was for the best.

He moved backward and closed the door, turning to face me. It didn't take a genius to see he was pissed as hell. Just about as pissed as I was.

"Some," he said. "Why?"

The letters went through my mind. My ancestors, all cursed to die at twenty-one. And though I wanted to, I couldn't deny the truth. I knew it was real; I *felt* it. The dead guy, my hair, the letters. It was all real. "Because my family is cursed. *I'm* cursed. Not 'cursed' as in my life sucks or I'm different, but seriously cursed." Yes, it was real, but it sure sounded like a bunch of baloney when said out loud. "Look, all I need is to be pointed in the right direction. I want this 'thing' gone, off me, whatever it is I need to do."

The anger of before gave way to defeat and a whole lot of pessimism. My shoulders slumped, and I grew as cold as the corpses in the morgue.

"How about this?" Sebastian said. "I know a person who can

lift curses. I'll show you the way to the most powerful voodoo priest in New 2. And after that, you let me show you around the Vieux Carré. Then we'll go together to quiz Josephine about your mother."

I was pretty sure I knew what I looked like: a cartoon hamster in the headlights. Totally not what I expected him to say, especially after I'd just implied he was one of the bad guys. "Uh . . ." What the hell was I supposed to say to that? "Okay?"

A grin split Sebastian's face, slicing two dimples into his cheeks.

Holy Mary Mother of God. I actually stopped breathing for a second.

"Good," he said, still smiling. "Let's get out of here. It's freezing."

Six

CRANK WAS RIGHT. THE NOVEM HAD CONCENTRATED MUCH, IF
not all, of their effort and money on rebuilding the French
Quarter, or the Vieux Carré, as Sebastian called it. As we ambled
down Bourbon Street, every building had been restored, every
windowpane, shutter, and iron railing refurbished. Even the
sidewalks, which Sebastian told me were known as banquettes,
had been repaired. Like every postcard image I'd ever seen of the
French Quarter, they left nothing out. The area thrived, too. This
was their moneymaker. This was where the tourists came, where
Mardi Gras still drew enormous crowds.

And Mardi Gras was in full swing, having begun on January 6. In a few weeks, it would end with the biggest parades and
balls on the night before Fat Tuesday in February. In the mean-

time, there were balls every weekend, local parades, and vendors selling masks and costumes like crazy.

The Quarter teemed with activity, a vibrant place with doors thrown open to bars, antique shops, restaurants, clubs, and bed-and-breakfasts. Mules plodded by pulling carriages. Musicians played on busy corners. And the only traffic was the occasional delivery truck—no personal vehicles allowed in the Quarter. "To preserve the ambiance and history," Sebastian explained.

"Voodoo Alley," he said as we turned onto Dumaine Street.

The street was a colorful mix of homes and businesses, mostly voodoo related. "The ones like those"—he pointed to a ground-floor shop filled with small pouches, spell packs, relics, statues, scarves, and handmade dolls—"those are tourist traps."

As we went by, a small walking tour exited the shop, the tour guide dressed like the old Voodoo Queen, Marie Laveau.

"Where are the real shops?" I stepped off the sidewalk and onto the street to go around the tour.

Sebastian shoved his hands into his pockets. "Back rooms, courtyards, private homes, the swamps ..."

We angled back onto the sidewalk, passing a long strip of houses on both sides of the street. The area became quieter, but no less colorful—the houses painted in the bright colors of the Caribbean. Long wooden shutters framed open windows, which allowed the breeze in from the river.

But even here in the residential space, voodoo was everywhere. Adorning every door, railing, and gate were beads, flowers, votive candles, gris-gris pouches, handmade dolls, beautiful scarves, trinkets, and effigies of saints.

Sebastian stopped in front of one such gate. The wrought iron whined as he pushed it open. We entered a tunnel, a dark space where the sound of our footsteps bounced off the vaulted brick ceiling of the courtyard passageway running between the West Indies–style homes on either side.

My eyes watered as we ventured from the darkness of the tunnel and into the bright light of a large walled courtyard. Water splashed from a fountain in the center and everywhere there were birds—chirping, fluttering, moving in the trees. Scarves and beads hung from the large banana tree in the back left-hand corner.

"This way," Sebastian said quietly.

I followed him along the brick path to a stone patio that butted up to the first floor of the house. Three sets of French doors ran the length of the ground floor. The middle set was open, held ajar by potted plants and a crude, life-size wood carving of the Virgin Mary, her neck draped with beads.

Incense clouded the room inside. Fine particles of dust and wisps of smoke floated in random shafts of sunlight. The room was packed with things. Weird things. Old things. Gaudy things. So many things that I found it hard to concentrate.

"Sebastian Lamarliere," said a deep, heavily accented Cajun voice with a slight singsong quality. A figure came around the corner in a thin, wide-sleeved robe that brushed the tops of long bare feet. Dark skin and eyes. Closely cropped gray, frizzy hair. Two large hoops in the ears. There were rings on the fingers of one hand and a bouquet of daisies in the other.

I was stumped.

It was the first time in my life I couldn't tell a person's gender. My eyes fell to the neck, looking for an Adam's apple, but it was swathed in a colorful scarf, the ends trailing down the back of the gown.

"Jean Solomon," Sebastian said with respect.

He said it in the French way. The French "Jean" was male. *Male it is, then.*

Jean went behind a long counter and retrieved a vase for the flowers. "These are for Legba," he said, smelling a daisy before snuggling it into the vase.

Jean beckoned for us to step closer; the warm wise eyes and gentle tone of voice made me a little more at ease. I gave him a small smile, not sure what to say, and it took several uncomfortable minutes before he slid the vase aside and propped his arms on the counter. "What interesting thing have you brought into my shop, Bastian?" His eyes squinted at me, bright with amusement, but deep and knowing and mysterious.

"Sebastian brought me here to see if you can lift my curse . . . an old one."

An eyebrow rose at my words, or the fact that I'd answered for Sebastian; I couldn't tell. "An old one, indeed." He rested his chin on one hand. "Love the moon tattoo. What is your name, *chère?*"

"Ari."

"And, what, Miss *Ar-eee*, will you offer the loa in return for removing this curse?"

I knew enough to know that loa were the spirits a voodoo priest called upon to aid him, and Legba was a spirit that acted as a guide between the priest and the spirit world. Or at least, that was how I thought it went. What I hadn't considered was payment. And I was running low on funds.

"I tell you what," Jean said, "we will see about this curse and the loa will tell you what they want for it, *c'est bon?*"

I released my breath. "Thanks." His wink brought a smile to my face and eased the tension from my shoulders. *Now we're getting somewhere.*

He moved around the counter, urging me and Sebastian into a large square room, ringed with items and chairs but empty in the center. On the far wall was a wide altar, caked with candle wax, small idols of voodoo and Christian religion, food, trinkets, and dried blood. There was a photograph of a woman in a turban and a large statue of Christ on the cross. Curled around the base of the statue was a yellow python. A small python, but size never really mattered when it came to snakes.

The blood drained from my face as the electric tingle of fear swamped me. My arms and legs went numb, and my heart began to pound like one of Sebastian's drums. I froze, unable to move another step. Distance. *Yes, keep your distance.*

"It's okay," Sebastian said, sensing my distress. "Snakes are used to help the priest focus and connect with the spirits."

"Come, come." Jean shut the French doors and then shuffled to the altar, gently picking up the snake and setting it on his shoulders. Its tail curled under his neck as he lit the altar candles.

All the hairs on the back of my neck lifted. Jean turned to us and took two steps closer. One more and I knew I'd run. I wouldn't be able to control it. The snake was staring straight at me.

But Jean stopped at the second step, took a deep breath, and closed his eyes. "Legba," he whispered reverently, reaching both hands up to stroke the snake. "Papa Legba, open the gate for me, so I can go through. When I return, I will honor the loa. *Papa Legba ouvri baye-a pou mwen, pou mwen pase. Le ma tounen, ma salyie lwa yo. Papa Legba ouvri baye-a pou mwen, pou mwen pase. Le ma tounen, ma salyie lwa yo.*"

Jean repeated his incantation over and over again until it

sounded like a song. Faster and faster. He swayed as he chanted the words, putting himself into a deep trancelike state. The snake moved back and forth with Jean, balancing in its creepy reptilian way, eyes never leaving me. Sebastian and I found ourselves swaying too.

Jean stopped suddenly, deathly still.

I almost jumped out of my skin.

Six seconds passed. I counted them, trying to calm my racing pulse, but it wasn't working. Slowly his eyes opened, and they were different from before. Milkier. He smiled and said a few unintelligible words, looking at us or beyond us, I wasn't sure.

"What do you seek?"

I swallowed hard, casting a quick glance at Sebastian. He looked as anxious as I did, and a little paler. I drew in a steadying breath, noticing that Jean's eyes and head had tipped back and were fixed on the ceiling fan. "Um." I cleared my throat. "I seek a way to remove my curse."

It was so fast I didn't even see his face tilt back down or his eyes move. They were on the ceiling and then suddenly they were on me. Too fast to be human. I froze. The snake held its head out and away from Jean's shoulder, intent on me.

And then all hell broke loose.

Jean or Papa Legba—whoever the hell he was now—yelled, jumping up and down as though he'd caught fire. The snake dropped to the floor and slithered underneath the altar, turning its head around to hiss at me. A furious argument erupted between Papa Legba and Jean Solomon. The same person. Two different voices.

I backed away slowly, catching bits and phrases in the broken English and French and whatever else they were speaking.

Sebastian reached out and grabbed my hand as Jean said to himself, "She cannot hurt—"

"Bah! Legba is not *scared*!" His head swung around and he ran right up to me, stretched out his neck, and stuck his face in mine. I couldn't move or breathe. "YOU DON'T FRIGHTEN *ME*!"

Blood vessels swelled on Jean Solomon's head. His face shook with rage. Then he straightened and marched back to the altar, gesturing wildly. "Dishonor, dishonor, dishonor!"

And then Jean's calm voice, "Shh. Shh. Shh . . ." Followed by unintelligible, soothing mumblings as Jean tried to placate the angry spirit.

More angry words.

And then Jean Solomon doubled over, and all was quiet except the blood hammering through my eardrums and the birds outside that began their songs once more. Goose bumps covered my skin. My grip on Sebastian's hand was brutal, but he didn't let go. Actually, he was holding on to mine just as hard as I held on to his.

Jean straightened; he looked confused, embarrassed, and a little frightened as he approached us. "You must go," he said, and the voice that came out was more feminine and tired.

"But—"

"I am sorry, Miss Ari, but the loa will not help you."

Desperation swept cold through my stomach. "Look, I can pay. I can get more money. Please, I need to know something, anything. What did he say?"

Jean ushered us to the French doors, pressing the handle so the doors would swing open. He held out a hand. "Please, go."

I hesitated, but Sebastian tugged on my hand. Jean kept his eyes on the floor as we went through the door, but once we were out into the courtyard, he surprised me by stepping out and shutting the door quietly behind him.

Jean's tone was low; obviously he didn't want to be heard. "I have dishonored my loa with your presence here. It was my fault, for I did not see you as you truly were until I joined with Legba. You must never come back here."

"Why? What do you mean?" My fists clenched at my sides. I wanted to scream in frustration. "What the hell is wrong with me?"

Sadness passed through his eyes. "I hope you never find out." And then he turned away, shaking his head.

"Please, Jean," I said, begging now. He saw my curse. He *knew* what it was; he was the *only* one who knew. "I need help."

Jesus Christ, I *hated* to beg. Hated it so much that it made my chest tight and sour.

Jean sighed, then shook his head again like he was about to do something he shouldn't. He leaned away from the door. "You want to know the past, what has been put on you? Grind a bone of Alice Cromley into powder, powder as fine as dust, and then you'll see. Those bones will tell you your story. Bastian knows, don't you?" Sebastian nodded, and Jean seemed satisfied. "Good luck, *chère*."

He went back inside and closed the door.

I turned to Sebastian. "Please tell me he's not serious."

Sebastian took my arm, leading me away from the house and back to the passageway. "Unfortunately, he's dead serious."

Figures.

I yanked my arm away and marched down the courtyard tunnel and back to Dumaine Street. I didn't bother waiting for Sebastian as I stormed out of the gate, letting it slam back on the lock, and headed south.

All I wanted was some normalcy in my life. That was all! Why was that so freaking hard to come by? *Why?*

Tears stung my eyes, stupid, burning tears that I swiped away with the back of my hand. A scream welled inside my chest, pushing against my heart and ribs, hurting like hell. I sniffed hard and—

A bright flash blinded me.

An intense bolt of pain sliced through my brain, making me scream, hands going to my head as I stumbled to my knees in the street. I doubled over, my elbows on the pavers, my fingers pulling at the roots of my hair as the pain mushroomed out to the very ends of my skull and then rebounded back in to do more damage. I screamed again as waves of agony flowed through my head.

It was too much . . . too much.

Hands curled around my shoulders, pulling me back, lifting me up off the ground.

My eyes opened but didn't see, too blinded by pain. The side of my wet face bumped against cloth. Sebastian's shirt. His smell. His voice, though I couldn't understand his words. His lips and warm breath were on my temple, talking softly. I turned into him, seeking solace, comfort, some kind of escape, but it still hurt. Every step he took vibrated fresh pain through my head.

And then, thank God, he stopped. He held me tight, wrapping his arms around me, leaning back. I held on, squeezing my eyes closed and locking myself away. But not alone. Thankfully, this time, not alone.

Seven

A MELLOW JAZZ TUNE PLAYED COMPANION TO THE STEADY thud of Sebastian's heart, the piano notes meandering through my waking mind like a tranquil breeze. Dull remnants of pain clung to the curve of my skull, a reminder of my breakdown in the middle of Dumaine Street and the arms that held me—that *still* held me.

The right side of my face pressed against the soft cotton of Sebastian's T-shirt, my ear over his heart. One of his hands cupped the back of my neck, his fingers tangled in my loose hair. His other hand was splayed on my lower back, palm against the bare skin where my shirt had ridden up. Warmth surrounded me. His warmth. His smell. His arms. His legs were braced on either side of me, my hip snuggled squarely against his crotch.

The more I woke, the more my rising pulse drowned out the beat of Sebastian's heart. A cool sensation swept into my stomach. Every nerve ending came alive from being that close . . . and being embarrassed as hell that I'd clung to him for this long.

Might as well get it over with.

Drawing in a subtle breath and biting down on my lip, I lifted my head and opened my eyes. Using both hands, one on Sebastian's chest and the other near his shoulder, I pushed myself to a sitting position between his legs as the weight of my hair fell around my face. I'd never had my hands on a guy like this. Never felt the warmth and the muscle and the give of skin beneath my palms.

Once I was up, my eyes landed on Sebastian. For once, I was glad that my hair was down and shielding my face. At least then, I could hide.

Sebastian's head rested back against the dark green seat, his body snuggled into the V of a corner booth. A bartender polished a bar top as a piano player played, and a waitress served drinks to the only other couple in the dark room. The front door was open to the street outside.

When I returned my gaze to Sebastian, his eyes were half-open and fixed on me in a quiet, unreadable way. The color seemed to smolder like smoke, a mist of gray and silver. His lips had become deep red in his relaxed state. His head still rested against the seat, and his pale throat bobbed in a faint swallow. I didn't move. I couldn't.

For once, I wasn't embarrassed that my hair was down. My mind became calm, totally at ease, though my body was another story. Blood thrummed through my veins at the speed of light. Small shafts of tingling energy shot out randomly from my stomach.

Sebastian lifted his hand and gently threaded his fingers through my hair. My heart thudded hard when he took the same hand and brought it to my cheek, sliding it through my hair and cupping my head, guiding me to him.

It was as though I still slept, still existed in dreamland.

And it seemed the same for him, because his body was completely at ease. There was no pause, no hesitation, just a slow unstoppable journey to his lips.

My stomach did a three-sixty as my lips hovered above his for a feathery moment, so close our breath mingled. Then my lips brushed his.

A shot of cool adrenaline swept through my system. The pressure of our lips increased. His parted. Mine followed. The slide of his tongue against mine made butterflies in my stomach.

Butterflies. Now I understood what that meant.

He pulled me closer, tighter, deepening the kiss, as though starving, yet taking the time to savor every second. I knew how to kiss, knew the mechanics involved, but this was the first time I'd ever lost myself, ever wanted it more than breathing, and wanted to keep doing it until time stood still and the earth faded away.

I was alive. Not just existing, but truly alive.

"Oh, shoot!" came a shocked voice at the other side of the table. I broke away with a gasp, just catching the waitress's grin. "Sorry, didn't mean to interrupt. I can come back later. . . ."

Sebastian straightened, rubbed a hand down his face, and then dragged his fingers through his hair. I cleared my throat, finally feeling that embarrassment I'd been missing earlier, though it did nothing to swamp the heat from our kiss, heat that felt insanely good and tense and enthralling all at the same time. "It's okay," I managed despite my ragged breathing. "I'd love some water, if you have any."

Of course they have water. What an asinine thing to say.

"Anything for you, Sebastian?"

"Water, too, Pam. Thanks."

Pam left the table as Sebastian's hands settled on my hips. "How are you feeling?" Pink blushed his cheeks for just a second. "I mean your head." He laughed at himself. "Does it still hurt?"

"No. It's fine. Thanks, though . . . for helping. Where are we?"

"Gabonna's. A block over from where you collapsed. I come here all the time. Does that happen a lot?"

"Does what happen a lot?"

One corner of his mouth lifted. "The screaming in the street. Falling to your knees. Crying . . ."

Honestly, I wasn't sure how to answer. I'd been having migraines more frequently lately, but nothing of *that* magnitude before. The waitress returned with the waters. I chugged half the glass. The cold liquid woke me up and cleared my head. I set the glass down and then twisted my hair into a knot.

"You should wear it down."

My cheeks were still warm, but I was smiling as I fixed my hair. "Is that a compliment?"

"It is. I like it. It's . . ."

"Weird? Bizarre? Different? Yeah, I get that all the time." I rolled my eyes, finishing.

"I was going to say pretty."

"Oh." Great. *Way to go, moron.* It was obvious that I sucked in the guy department. I hadn't exactly had much practice with the whole flirting and boy thing. Most of my time had been spent avoiding guys or fighting with the ones who refused to *let* me avoid them.

"Sorry," I said, deciding to be honest. "Look, I don't really do the guy thing. Or the kissing thing . . ."

"So no boyfriends back home?"

I couldn't tell if he thought it was funny or if he really wanted to know. Looked like a mix of both. "No."

"Why's that?"

"Well, guess I haven't come across many who can think beyond sports, hormones, and partying."

"And you don't do those things?"

I shrugged. "Maybe I would have in another life. The things that are important to the kids my age stopped being important to me a long time ago, or never were." I made a half bow. "Behold, a product of underfunded, nobody-gives-a-shit social services."

He laughed. "It's almost lunchtime. And as good as the food is here, I have something else in mind. What do you say we get out of here?"

"What exactly do you have in mind?"

"Beignets."

My stomach rumbled at the idea. "Now *that* I can do." Sebastian returned my grin with one of his own. And then it dawned on me that we were sitting there smiling at each other like two idiots. I broke eye contact and scooted from the bench, grabbing my backpack as Sebastian dug into his front pocket for a few dollars to leave on Pam's table.

Clouds had gathered outside, but nothing to suggest a storm brewing. The shade was a godsend, because I was pretty sure, after my migraine from hell, that my head wouldn't be able to handle bright light anytime soon.

Outside Gabonna's, Sebastian whistled to one of the carriages plodding down Saint Ann Street. The driver waved, made a U-turn in the street, and then pulled up alongside us. "*Bonjour, mes amis.* Where can me and Miss Praline take you on this fine day?"

He had an infectious white smile, which I returned as I climbed into the back of the creaking carriage. I hadn't imagined my foray into New 2 would involve a tourist ride through the French Quarter, but I was glad for the distraction . . . and the company. "Jackson Square," Sebastian told the driver as he sat down beside me.

"You hear that, Miss Praline? Jackson Square." The driver flicked the reins over her large rump, and Miss Praline lengthened her stride.

We wouldn't get there in record time, but I supposed that was the point; go slow and savor the sights and sounds of the French Quarter. Sebastian's shoulder leaned into mine, so I took his cue and relaxed against him. Weird, but I liked it.

I needed a break like this, needed to forget all the dark things for a little while, so I listened to the driver point out places of interest and followed Sebastian's finger whenever he showed me something he thought I'd like.

"And this," the driver said as we rode slowly past a three-story house on the corner with double porches and wrought-iron railings, "was said to be the home of Alice Cromley."

The name, the same name Jean Solomon had said, prickled my skin. I exchanged a quick glance with Sebastian, and then bent forward to ask the driver, "Who was Alice Cromley?"

The driver angled in his red padded seat, eyes alight and eager to tell a story. "Who was Alice Cromley? Now ain't *that* a question? Alice Cromley was a quadroon, the greatest Creole beauty the Vieux Carré had ever seen. Why, she had a bevy of suitors, but she knew about them too, ya know? Knew things a mistress ought *not* know, if ya get my meanin'." He chuckled. "You see, Alice Cromley was what they call clairvoyant. Made a fortune telling people what they wanted to know. And she was never wrong unless she *meant* to be. One day, she just up and vanished. Just like that. Couple weeks later, they found two bodies floatin' in the Mississippi. Hard to identify 'cause, well, they'd been there for a while. But some say one of the poor departed souls was wearing Alice's finest gown." He laughed and clucked to the slow-moving mule. "One of her lovers made her a tomb in a cemetery round here. Nobody knows which one. It's said he placed both bodies inside, figuring one of them had to be his beloved Alice." The man shrugged. "Guess he figured one out of two ain't bad."

And her bones, according to Jean Solomon, could tell me the past. *Yeah. Fat chance of that.*

The carriage rolled by St. Louis Cathedral and into Jackson Square.

I forgot about Alice Cromley for the moment to admire the tall spire of the cathedral as Miss Praline pulled us down the length of the Pontalba Apartments. They were the oldest apartments in the United States, with long, cast-iron balconies, red brick, and ground-floor stores. The statue of Andrew Jackson atop his horse stood in the center of the square. There was energy here, energy that seeped into my soul and gave me a much-needed boost. Colorful. Vibrant. Beautiful. There were fortune-tellers, jewelry makers, artisans, musicians . . . it was an eclectic mix of everything.

Then it was toward the Riverwalk and Decatur Street, where the carriages parked.

After tipping the driver, Sebastian helped me down from the carriage and kept hold of my hand as we headed across the street to Café Du Monde. I didn't pull my hand away; it felt good. And if he wasn't letting go, neither was I.

The smell of freshly baked bread and coffee made my stomach grumble again as we found a seat outside under the green-and-white-striped awning.

Sebastian ordered a plate of beignets and two coffees. I was too busy people watching and admiring all the details of the square, surprised by how much green there was.

"I bet your mom brought you here." Sebastian broke through my sightseeing.

"Why do you say that?"

He shrugged, a small smile playing at the corners of his dark lips. "If she lived in New Orleans, she would've come here. It's kind of a fact of life."

That was probably true. I wasn't even a local, and I knew that everyone went to Café Du Monde. "You're right," I responded softly, looking around at the café. "She probably did bring me here." If only I could remember. What would it have been like? Coming here with my mom, sitting at one of these tables . . .

"So, you want to find Alice Cromley?" Sebastian asked, changing the subject. He tried to hide his amusement, but lost that battle pretty quick.

"Yeah. No, thank you. I think I'd rather take my chances with your grandmother than rob some woman's grave and grind up her bones." A small shudder went through me as the waiter returned with our order.

"Scared?" He poured cream into his coffee. "You haven't lived until you go grave robbing."

A laugh spurted through my lips right before they touched the rim of my coffee cup. "Whatever you say." The hot liquid was just the thing on a cool January day in the French Quarter. After a few sips, I set the cup down and picked up a beignet. It steamed as I pulled it apart.

"Suit yourself," Sebastian went on. "Dub is one of the best robbers around. You should see some of the things he's found."

"Dub. Dub robs graves. Are you shitting me?" The beignet melted in my mouth. I groaned—damn, they tasted good.

"A lot of kids do it. We all have to make money somehow. Crank runs the mail. I work for the Novem. Henri clears buildings of rats and snakes. And Dub robs tombs and sells stuff to tourists and antique shops."

"That's pretty sick."

His eyebrow lifted in agreement. "Well, we don't exactly spend our time thinking about sports, hormones, or partying, either." He made the same half bow I had earlier. "Behold, a product of New 2." He laughed. The sound was deep and infectious, and there were those incredible dimples again. . . .

"So tell me about the nine, the Novem." I took another bite, wanting to change the subject from corpses and graveyards, and definitely from my growing infatuation with my tour guide. "Why do they still act so reclusive?"

"Not reclusive. They just don't care about the outside world like you all do."

"What do they care about, then?"

"Preserving the city"—he spoke between bites and chewing—

"the history of our people and those like us, offering refuge to like-minded individuals, a place where you're not judged or turned into a lab experiment."

"Lab experiment?"

He propped both elbows on the table. "New 2 is home to a lot of what the Novem call 'gifted' people. What do you think would happen if Violet or Dub—or I—lived beyond The Rim?"

Easy. "If they couldn't hide their abilities, life wouldn't be so kind," I answered in a quiet voice, thinking of my own experiences.

"Exactly. New 2 is a place where you don't have to hide, but if you want to, that's okay too. No one is going to judge you because you're different. That's what the Novem wanted all along."

My heart skipped a beat. "Because they're different too." They weren't just old families with old money, they were different. *Doué*, as Dub called them. Sebastian nodded. "And the rest of your family, the Arnauds, are like you? Able to hypnotize people?"

His chewing slowed as he thought over his answer. "They're able to do that, yes."

I wanted to believe him, to believe that the Novem wasn't behind the man who'd attacked me in Covington, that they were on my side and were actually a decent bunch of people.

But I'd learned over the years that it was better to suspect the worst. That was a hell of a lot better than trusting someone, giving them the benefit of the doubt, and then having them stab you in the heart.

We sipped our coffee and finished the plate of beignets. Sebastian paid the bill. "So you think you're ready to see Josephine?"

I stood and tossed my backpack over one shoulder. "I guess now is as good a time as any."

Eight

Sebastian filled me in as we walked across the square. Flanking each side of St. Louis Cathedral were two enormous historic buildings. The Presbytère, on the right, had been converted into the Novem's swanky private school/college, which Sebastian was supposed to attend but ditched on a regular basis. And the building on the left was the Cabildo, which remained a museum as it had since pre–New 2 days, but the second and third floors had been taken over by the Novem as their official place of business. This was also where they held the Council of Nine meetings, attended only by the head of each family.

And each family had apartments and private offices in the two Pontalba apartment buildings that ran along both sides of the Square.

Apparently, Jackson Square was Novem central.

With every step across the square and toward the building, my muscles became more tense. I craned my neck to stare again at the tall spire of St. Louis Cathedral. "So how far back does your family go exactly?"

"The first Arnaud came to New Orleans in 1777. He was the third son of a noble family from the Narbonne area in France."

A trio of musicians played near the benches in front of the cathedral. The wind picked up, and low clouds blocked the sun. The air turned damp and cold with the threat of rain. A few drops started to fall just as we ducked under one of the archways of the Cabildo building.

A hollow, hushed atmosphere greeted us on the inside. There were a few permanent exhibits, but I didn't exactly have time to look around as Sebastian ushered me to a flight of stairs.

The second-floor landing had been retrofitted to resemble a fancy office building, complete with a central receptionist desk. Sebastian let go of my hand as the guy behind the desk glanced up, recognized him, and gave a faint nod before returning to his work.

Our footsteps echoed loudly over the polished wood floors as we made our way down the long gallery fronting the building. The stormy light from outside poured through the arched windows, illuminating the space in an eerie glow. Halfway down, a hallway intersected with the gallery.

Sebastian turned. I followed. No windows. No artificial light. Just a corridor that got darker and darker the farther in we went.

We stopped at the last door on the right. My pulse drummed steady in my ears. Josephine Arnaud had paid my mother's co-pay. They had to have known each other. She might even know my father. I swallowed the lump in my throat, trying not to get too hopeful. But I was so close.

The waiting room we entered was just as old and sacred as the rest of the building. The furniture looked way too expensive to sit on, and the paintings on the walls were probably worth a few million. I wished there was some sort of piped-in music, something other than this ominous quiet.

A man looked up from his desk as we approached. He was handsome, in his thirties probably, and *not* what I'd picture a secretary looking like. Dark brown hair pulled back into a ponytail. A widow's peak. Very classic features.

He pursed his lips, eyes narrowing on Sebastian. "Have you come to your senses yet, Bastian?"

Sebastian stiffened. "My senses are right where they should be, Daniel."

"I hardly call ditching classes and living in some rotting old Garden Dis—"

"Just tell Josephine we're here."

Daniel's dark eyes held Sebastian's for a long, tense second before they fell on me. "So you found her," he said, sizing me up and probably wondering what the hell the old lady wanted me for anyway. "Madame will be pleased. You can go in." He picked up the phone and mumbled quietly as we crossed the room to a set of double doors.

Sebastian turned to me, giving me an eye roll that said, *This is about to be loads of fun* before pushing open the door. I drew in a deep breath and prepared to meet the person who might have all the answers.

A raven-haired woman put down the phone and slowly stood, tugging down the bottom edge of a rose-colored blazer over a matching skirt, a crisp white blouse underneath. Her dark hair was up in a twist, and she wore pearl earrings and a cameo necklace. Very old money. Very old world. And, from the looks of her, very *not* a grandma.

"*Bonjour, Grandmère.*" Sebastian leaned in to kiss both sides of her cheeks.

My eyelids fell closed for a moment, and then I shook my head, wanting to laugh. Really, how much more screwed up could this get? That woman had to be in her early twenties. There was no way in hell she was his grandmother. Any fool with half a brain could see that.

Sebastian moved back. Josephine's gaze zeroed in on me.

He'd lied. He'd fed me a bunch of bullshit and I'd believed

him. God, how stupid could I be? All I felt was idiocy, idiocy for believing some jerk of a guy. And why? Because he was cute, because he had shown some interest in me? "Whatever," I muttered, then spun on my heel and marched to the door, trying like mad not to feel hurt.

I didn't know what game he was playing, but I was done.

"Ari."

I didn't stop. Sebastian's hand closed around my arm. I whirled on him, fist clenched and wanting to take a swing. "Is this some kind of game to you, Sebastian? What, you had a free day and nothing to do, so why not mess around with the new girl? Have some fun? See how far you could lead me on? Get off me." I wrenched my arm away, not meeting those false gray eyes. "Just forget it." I made for the door.

He appeared in front of me, blocking the door.

I gasped, drawing up short, my face draining of blood. He'd moved *way* too fast.

Somewhere I heard my brain telling me to run, to hit him and make for the stairs, but I couldn't move.

His eyes held worry and regret, and maybe even a little pleading. His jaw flexed with frustration. "I'm sorry, Ari," he said under his breath. "I thought"—he rubbed a hand down his face—"I thought you'd be okay with it. Look at what you've seen so far. Remember what I told you in the café? About the *doué*, about being different? I wasn't lying. We *are* different." His eyes rolled to the ceiling. Both his hands clamped onto my biceps. "I'm trying to help you. I swear to you, she is my grandmother."

I took a step back and blinked hard, trying to shake away the mental fuzziness that was invading my head. Yeah, I'd been handling all the weird shit pretty well so far. So sue me. Now it was falling down like a freaking deluge and I couldn't escape it, couldn't put it all into a neat little compartment and ignore it. "What exactly are you?"

A lock of black hair fell over his eye, and he shoved it back with a deep sigh. His mouth opened, but nothing came out. His jaw went tight, and it seemed like he truly didn't know how to answer my question.

"He is an Arnaud," came a sultry, French-accented voice.

Sebastian's lips stretched into a grim line, as though he wished he was anything *but* an Arnaud.

"Come, sit down. Both of you," she said.

After a good glare at Sebastian, I turned and went to one of two empty chairs in front of Josephine's desk. Fine. Whatever was going on . . . didn't really matter. What did matter was getting answers about my mother. After that, I was out of there.

"Well," she began, scrutinizing me from head to toe, "except for that mark on your cheek, you look very much like your mother."

My eyes went wide. One hand gripped the back of the chair

and the other went to my stomach. Those words sent a tidal wave of shock through me. I had fuzzy memories, sure, but always questioned them. Always wondered.

Finally a question of mine had been answered, and it left me with an odd sense of happiness and hurt.

"Please sit." Josephine sat back in her own chair and studied me with a calculating look.

Breathe. Out of the corner of my eye, I saw Sebastian take a seat. My pulse was going too fast, and my limbs had gone weak. Maybe sitting down was a good idea.

"When Rocquemore House called me, I didn't believe it. But"—Josephine spread out her hands and smiled, which obviously was a rare event, because it looked like her skin was about to crack—"look at you. Here you are."

"So you knew about Rocquemore. You knew my mother was there."

"Your mother fled New Orleans against my advice. It took a few months, but it wasn't difficult to find her."

"And then you just left her there."

"What would you have suggested, child? Her mind was slipping away. She needed constant monitoring. The hospital was the best place for her. Unfortunately, by the time we found her, you were already lost in the system, or else you would have had a home here with us."

Sebastian let out a small snort.

"How did you know my mother?"

"Eleni came to me for help a few months before the hurricanes struck. Your mother was a very special woman, Ari. You must know this already, *oui*?"

"If by 'special' you mean cursed, then yeah, I know."

Josephine shrugged like it was tomatoes or tom-ah-toes.

"And my father?"

"Your father was a secret that Eleni kept to herself."

The bitch was lying. And she wasn't trying to hide it either. I crossed my arms over my chest. "And who are you exactly?"

"I am Josephine Isabella Arnaud. Daughter of Jacques Arnaud, founder of this family, the first of us to step foot in New Orleans."

I laughed, sharp and loud, an on-the-verge-of-a-mental-breakdown kind of laugh. "So you're the daughter of a man who came here in 1777? So that'd make you what? Three hundred plus years? You sure you shouldn't be at Rocquemore yourself?"

A throaty chuckle rumbled in Josephine's throat. "You have more spirit than she did. More . . . *attitude*."

Frustration welled in my chest with every passing second. "Why did you help my mother?"

"She was afraid. Alone. The only one of her kind, she said. I sensed she was different, but not until later did I truly understand the magnitude of her power."

"Which was?"

"I want to help you, Ari. There are people out there who would see you dead for what is inside you. Your mother should have stayed in New Orleans like I advised, but she panicked when the storms came. She didn't believe I could protect her, that we all, combined, could protect this city. But we did. And now we own it. She might still be alive if she'd stayed." She fiddled with the pen on her desk for a moment. "I have asked to see you to offer my protection while you're in our city. Together we will delve into your past and uncover this gift you have been given. But in return, you must grant your allegiance to me, a blood oath to the Arnaud family and no other."

"Was that what you asked of my mother? You weren't just helping out of the goodness of your heart?"

Josephine laughed. "I do not have a heart, my dear. Just ask my grandson." Sebastian's response was a smirk. "Do we have an agreement, child?"

"Will you give your word to lift my curse?"

"The power of the nine families can do anything. And *oui*, I give you my word."

I didn't plan on being in New 2 for very long after this *thing*, this curse my mother had died from, was out of my life for good. I had no intention of delving into my past with Josephine, but she didn't need to know that. I didn't trust a word uttered from her perfect lips. But I couldn't deny the fact that Josephine's name was on those hospital records. She *had* known my mother. There *had* been a disappearing dead guy who tried to kill me. Did I believe Josephine could erase this curse? Doubtful. But I was here now. There was no one else to make the attempt, and I didn't have a problem with flat-out lying to get her cooperation. "Fine. You lift my curse and I'll give you my oath."

"Give me two days to arrange the ritual. You will remain under the watchful eye of the Arnaud family. Etienne will be your guard. And you may stay—"

Sebastian shot to his feet. "The hell she's staying with you."

"Your thoughts or desires hold very little significance in my decision making, Sebastian."

"Etienne is an asshole."

Josephine ignored the outburst, propped both arms on her desk, and eyed Sebastian thoughtfully. "What, pray tell, would you have me do?"

"Not burden her with Etienne, for one."

I finally stood. Whatever. They could stay here all day and fight it out. "Thanks for the offer, but I can take care of myself. I'll need to call my foster parents and let them know I'll be staying a little longer."

The only sound in the room was the faint rumble of thunder in the distance. "Fine," Josephine said at last. "Go. I have work to do. Sebastian will watch over you. Daniel will help you with your call." She turned her attention to the files on her desk, but then paused. "I will expect you in two days' time."

I was trembling by the time Daniel made the call to Memphis. The Novem had working phones. And probably Internet, too.

Daniel handed me the phone. On the fourth ring, Casey picked up. "Sanderson Bail and Bonds, this is Casey."

I walked to the far wall. Sebastian waited by the door, leaning his back against it, arms crossed over his chest and impatient as hell to leave.

"Casey. It's me."

"Jesus Christ, Ari. Where are you? Bruce keeps trying your cell and all he gets is voice mail. We thought you'd be driving back by now." She paused, and I could picture her—the two lines between her eyebrows deepening with worry, tucking her shoulder-length red hair behind one ear. "Is everything okay?"

"Everything is fine. I met someone who knew my mother. She wants me to stay for a few days. *I* want to stay for a few days."

"Oh. Well …" Her long pause told me I'd completely thrown her. "You know I want this for you, Ari. And I won't stand in your way if this is what you want. But I am responsible for you. Is she there? Can I speak to her?"

I winced. "Sure. But before you freak out . . ." *Deep breath.* "I'm in New 2. And I'm sorry. I know you didn't want me going alone, but I had a lead, and it was just a quick trip and then I met Josephine and . . ." I paused for air, suddenly not knowing what to say next, only knowing that I'd blown it and lied, lied to the first set of foster parents who actually gave a damn.

Silence on the other end.

Finally Casey's exhale wafted through the phone. "I guess I had a feeling you might go after finding out about the hospital. Look, I get it, I really do. But you can't go running off without letting us know where you are. You're not eighteen yet. Bruce and I, we care what happens to you. I know that's probably hard to believe sometimes, but—"

"No," I cut her off. "I know you care. I screwed up. I'm sorry."

"Well, besides Bruce making you clean the office bathroom and do some sparring, I think we're okay. You know how he is about hard work making one think. Just . . . don't shut us out, okay? It doesn't solve anything, doesn't help anything."

"Okay." *I'm sorry. So sorry.* Didn't matter how many times I told her, or told myself, I knew I'd never be able to relate how bad I felt inside.

"I've got an appointment in five. Let me talk to this Josephine person."

◊   ◊   ◊

Sebastian was right behind me on the stairs, yelling at me to wait, but I didn't wait. To hell with him.

Anger and humiliation coursed through my blood. Anger at him, at Josephine, and at myself for lying. I was shit. Smelly, stinking shit, but what other kind was there really? Bruce was going to freak out when he found out. And Casey, her disappointment . . . God, that stung. I'd rather have her scream at me than just accept what I'd done, be understanding, and try to move on. I didn't deserve it. And the worst part about it, I'd broken their trust.

By the time I burst through the ground-floor door and out into the wet street, I was so mad I could've screamed.

A fine drizzle fell. The musicians had retired and the street was empty. Lights from the ground-floor stores of the Pontalba apartments glowed warm in the gray mist, making the area seem totally desolate.

I paced in the middle of the street, grateful for the chill, wondering if the steam coming off me was from body heat or pure, white-hot anger, which I turned on Sebastian. "What the hell are you? And don't change the fucking subject, or offer one of your vague-ass replies. I'm serious, Sebastian; I don't know how much more of this I can take."

I waited, hands on hips, watching him as his stiff posture gave way. "My mother was an Arnaud," he said. "But no matter what they say, I am more like my father." A muscle flexed in his jaw. "The nine families are divided into three groups. The Cromleys, Hawthornes, and Lamarlieres are witches of great power." He winced at the word "witches," looking like he'd rather have his teeth pulled without an ounce of Novocain. He tilted his face to the rain and took one more deep breath. "The Ramseys, Deschanels, and Sinclairs are all some form of demigod or shape-shifter. And the Arnauds, Mandevilles, and Baptistes are what you might call . . . vampires."

A slow blink was my only reaction.

The rest happened on the inside, the sink in my stomach, the cold freeze in my veins, and the realization that every word he said was true.

Really. It all fit. People beyond The Rim just laughed and shook their heads at the reports of paranormal activity, at the crazy claims of vampires and ghosts and other sightings in New 2. And me, with my curse. The kids on First Street. Sebastian and his ability to make those two women complete robots . . .

"You're a vampire." I laughed.

Yeah, and you watched a guy disappear into smoke, Ari.

"Half," he came back, as if there was a huge difference. "My father wasn't a vampire. He was a Lamarliere. I'm not some three-hundred-year-old pervert who kisses teenage girls, okay? I'm the same age as you. Born just like you."

He threw his hands up, gave me a look that said, *I know you think I'm crazy*, and then turned and marched down the middle of the street. Raindrops trickled down the side of my face. Ahead of him the French Quarter seemed lost in clouds and mist. Then suddenly he spun around, walking backward for a few steps, throwing his arms wide and shouting in frustration, "Welcome to New 2!"

He was in pain, and I didn't know why. He turned once more and hunched his shoulders against the drizzle. My heart worked overtime. My body was trembling uncontrollably, from the cold and from his words.

It shouldn't surprise me. It shouldn't. Especially after living with my own weirdness, and hearing all the theories and stories that had gone around about the Novem. And the curse. The kids in the Garden District.

What are you going to do, Ari? Run away? Act like you're all normal and can't handle weird shit like this? Or stay and cope and figure out what you are?

I paced in the street like a caged lion, back and forth, my eyes on Sebastian's form blending into the mist. I bit the inside of my cheek until blood hit my tongue and stung some humanity into me, some *realness*. These people still bled. They still died. They still loved, hurt, and wanted to survive. And so did the *doué*, the gifted ones. So did the Novem.

"Sebastian!"

I sprinted down the street.

He walked a few more steps before turning around, the rain coming down hard now. I didn't have a clue what I was doing or why. But I launched myself into him, wrapping my arms around him and holding on tight.

At first he remained stiff, through shock or anger, I didn't know, but then he squeezed me back, pulling me even closer, tighter, until his nose was buried against my neck.

Finally, after we were soaked through, he lifted his head and stared down at me, his hands cupping my face. "I thought you'd tell me to fuck off, and you'd leave. I thought every word I spoke was the last time I'd see you."

"Please. I can deal. Do you have any idea how screwed up I am?"

His crooked smile transformed his face. "Yeah. I've got some idea."

My belly went warm again. Sebastian kissed me, his lips wet from the rain.

Nine

"WE'VE MADE THIS AREA HOME SINCE THE BEGINNING. WHEN the hurricanes came, the families put their differences aside, combined their power, and protected as much of the city as they could. The Vieux Carré. The Garden District. The business district took a pretty big hit, which is why most of it is still in ruins. After it was all over, the heads of each family formed the council and began putting old grudges aside and talking. And once it was obvious the government didn't have the capacity to rebuild, they pooled their resources and bought the land. The city has been theirs ever since. They control everything—banking, real estate, tourism, trade . . . everything."

I listened, sipping on hot tea from a to-go cup as Sebastian spoke. After the rain had turned heavy, we'd raced to the sidewalk and found a small bookstore and café.

Sebastian's voice was quiet and his face pale, the gray eyes a stark and silvery contrast against his wet black hair and dark red lips. I could look at him forever. But that was something he'd never, *ever* know.

"There are other things living in this city and the outskirts," he continued. "The Novem offers refuge to anyone or anything so long as they stick to their laws and don't draw attention to themselves. Not everyone who lives here is different. Regular people live here too."

My fingers cradled the hot cup, and my stomach clenched. "So your mom was . . ."

"A vampire?" he answered with a laugh that sounded like he didn't believe it himself. "Yeah. And Josephine's only daughter."

"I always thought vampires were made, not born. That they couldn't have kids."

"That's what most people think." He smiled and gave a small shrug. "We don't exactly see the need to enlighten the outside world. It's pretty basic. We're not an entirely separate species or anything; we just branched off the human evolutionary tree a long time ago and evolved differently. You'd be surprised how many branches there are. But yeah, vampires can be made or born. The made ones are called Turned—basically humans turned into vampires."

"And the kids?"

"Kids are pretty rare. It's not easy for vamps to have children, but it happens sometimes. The kids grow up normally, but when they reach adulthood, their bodies stop aging. That's why most Born vamps look to be in their early twenties." He went to say more, but then hesitated and shook his head. "You sure you want to know all this?"

"Yeah. It's interesting." I gave a small laugh. "In a mind-blowing sort of way."

"Just be glad you didn't have to take Mr. Fry's molecular biology class, wherein all things human and *doué* are explained, all the way down to the genome level."

"Total snooze-fest, huh?"

"Yeah." He grew quiet.

I bit my lip, thinking over Sebastian's words for a moment. "But you're only half vampire?"

He propped his elbows on the table and leaned in. "I'll give you the short version. You've got full-blooded children, who are called Bloodborn. They're seen as nobility; they're the most powerful and the most annoying. I'm talking egos the size of Mount Everest. The children of a human and a vampire are called Dayborn. There are different traits among them, different strengths and weaknesses. Dayborns don't need blood to survive like Bloodborns do. Though there is a moment as they hit adulthood where the urge is there. If they take blood," he added, shrugging, "they'll need it from then on just like a Bloodborn would."

"Do they usually? Take it, I mean?"

Sebastian nodded, his expression going dim and the volume of his words lowering. "Blood is hard to resist for any vampire, no matter their birth."

The weight of his admission sat between us for a long moment. I cleared my throat. "And that's what you are, Dayborn?"

He glanced away. His Adam's apple moved with a tight swallow. "No. My other half is Lamarliere. So not quite human, either. A witch's DNA is slightly different, just like vamps and shifters, but they only tend to pass their power down maternally, through the female line."

"So . . . that would make you what, then?"

"I've always been partial to freak of nature."

"Ha," I shot back, smiling. "That one's mine."

He dipped his head, as though giving up his claim on the title. "Seriously, though, when I was little, my dad snuck me to a hidden library in the Presbytère, one that the students never see. One that houses some *really* old shit. He took out this stone tablet and said it told the story of a child like me. My dad called her Mistborn."

"Mistborn," I repeated.

"Yeah. Because mist hides what's inside. And that's sort of how I am. A big question mark, see? No one can say what traits, curses, or needs I'll have until they manifest themselves. Some have needed blood to survive. Some never need it. Some can control it."

"Oh." Warmth crept up my neck, and I shifted in my chair. "So, um, which type are you?"

He shook his head and then stared beyond my shoulder, his gaze unreadable. "I don't know. No telling if or when the need will strike."

Well, that was comforting. My grip on the cup increased. "How many of you are there?"

He held up both hands and sat back. "You're looking at it."

"One. You're the only one."

"In North America, yeah. There are a couple more in the world, I think. Like I said, *we* don't happen very often."

"But what about Crank? She's your sister."

"Jenna isn't my sister, Ari. Not by blood."

"But . . ." I frowned.

He paused, thinking of the right words. "This place kind of makes you band together. You find others like yourself, others you know you can trust with your life, and you become family. That's what Violet is learning. That's why she stays now more than she goes." He shrugged, seeming uncomfortable with sharing so much and showing that he had a heart. "Jenna lost her parents and then her brother. It damaged her a little. When I found her, she was still sitting by his body. She thought I was him, and she went with me. I never tried to reason with her. Never saw the need to hurt her more. This is how she copes. She makes up things."

My chest tightened at his words. "How did he die?"

"Not sure. I found them in Midtown, the business district. The ruins. You should never go there at night, or alone no matter what time of day it is. That place is a haven for predators. I think that's why the Novem leaves it alone. They'd rather let the bad among us have the ruins than run the risk of them branching out into the Quarter or the Garden District."

He gazed out the rain-streaked window. "Looks like the rain has stopped." I didn't press him, and part of me knew it was because I didn't want to answer *his* questions when the time came. Maybe he'd show me the same courtesy. "You want to go to the market? I told the others I'd pick up food for dinner."

"Sure."

It was a short walk from the café, across the square, and to the French Market near the river. The sun came out as we entered the covered space. Tourists and locals had taken refuge from the rain, and the inside teemed with shoppers. The bright colors of vegetables and fruits, meats and cheeses, plants and garden ornaments occupied the space. Sebastian seemed to know what he was shopping for, but I chose a slower route, taking things in, browsing, looking at everyone and wondering who was human and who was not, wondering if—because I was *doué*—I could somehow tell the difference.

But no one stood out. New 2 was also a haven for pagans, Wiccans, and alternative lifestyles, so the cut of one's clothes or the jewelry pierced into one's skin didn't mean anything.

Giving up on my detection attempts, I browsed the stalls, taking in the scents of coffee and bread, of freshly cut flowers, and even the smell of the river, which wound through the market on an occasional breeze.

Mardi Gras booths had been set up to sell beads, masks, and costumes. Soon I found myself lost in a rainbow of colors and tight spaces, leaving Sebastian behind as he haggled over a bag of potatoes. The Mardi Gras beads were cold to the touch and flowed through my hand like water. The masks were beautiful, yet haunting and seductive.

A black velvet, gold-lined mask with small, furry black feathers caught my eye, and I immediately thought of Violet. I knew she'd love it, and I could picture it sitting atop her head. I dropped my backpack onto the floor and pulled out some cash.

At another stall, I bought beignets for Dub and Henri and a metal mind puzzle for Crank. Once that was done, I wondered what Sebastian might like, and if it would seem weird to everyone that I'd bought gifts in the first place.

Near the end of the long covered building, I browsed through a line of scarves blowing in the breeze. A strong gust went through, causing a section of scarves to wrap around my face and neck as I turned back to search for Sebastian. I spun out of their satiny caress and ran straight into a hard body.

"Oh. Sorry."

No response. No movement or the slightest flinch. My stomach dropped as foreboding stilled my heart. I glanced up.

Another black T-shirt. Another blond-headed giant. Another freaking-ass blade and shield.

My hand itched for the gun in my waistband, but there were people nearby. I hesitated, caught totally off guard.

I shouldn't have hesitated.

He grabbed my arm, pivoted, and jerked me out the end of the market.

"Hey!" I pulled back, my adrenaline spiking. "Sebastian!" I dug in my heels and pulled hard, using my other hand to unwrap his tight fingers. "Let me go!" He didn't, and I almost tripped when he yanked me harder. He had both of my wrists pinned in his hard grip, dragging me toward the river.

My eyes met the vendor in the scarf booth. The way he slunk back into the darkness of the booth, eyes down, made me wonder if this was a normal thing. Couldn't be. I yelled again, hoping to alert the tourists, but we were several feet away already and the boats on the water and the noise from the market must've drowned out my screams.

Seeing the water gave me a sudden, horrifying thought—he was going to drown me. I pulled hard, leaning down to bite his hand. He let up enough for one of my hands to escape, and I used it to punch him hard, connecting with his left cheekbone.

I pulled the gun from my waistband, but as I brought it up, his free hand slapped down on my wrist, holding my arm out to the side, the gun away from its intended target. I struggled, but was no match for his size and strength. Time to rethink my strategy. Our gazes locked. My mouth curved into a smile, throwing him off guard for a split second; at the same time I raised my knee and slammed it into his groin. His hold on my wrists increased, but he groaned and bent over. Perfect position for me to knee him in the face. Which I did.

He cried out and cursed in the same odd language the other guy had used. Then he straightened, face red, nose trickling blood, veins engorged in his temples. I saw the head butt coming, but didn't have a chance in hell to stop it.

My vision wavered and then bled into blackness.

◊　◊　◊

The soft hum of an engine. The rhythmic rocking and splashing against the fiberglass siding of a boat brought me slowly back to reality.

The bristles of the blue turf that lined the floor of the boat had scratched my cheekbone raw. A fine, wet spray blew over me, cold and refreshing, giving me the extra jolt I needed to clear my head. I didn't move, but saw the legs standing at the controls as the boat bounced over the waves of what had to be the Mississippi.

My gun was gone. I didn't need to move to feel the absence of its metal grip against my skin, but at least my backpack had made the trip. It sat on the bench near the controls. Inside was the dagger. And if I didn't have my gun, the dagger was the next best thing.

As soon as I straightened, bracing my hands on the turf for balance, a throb of pain mushroomed through my head. *Breathe. Breathe through it.* The nauseating motion of the boat wasn't helping my chances of getting to my feet. *Shit.* I eyed the backpack, deciding the best course of action would be to nix the dagger attempt and knock the kidnapper off the boat using surprise and my body weight.

But trying to stand on a moving boat after you'd been head-butted by a two-hundred-pound asshole with a lead skull was like trying to ride a bike blindfolded through six inches of mud.

The boat hit a patch of calm water and slowed, coasting. I knew I'd have only a second before he checked on me. I pushed myself to my feet and lunged just as he turned.

The boat dipped in the front as it came to a stop. The force sent me barreling straight into his open arms, which wrapped around my torso as the boat glided to a small dock. Over his shoulder, the setting sun blinded me for a second as it sank down into the black horizon of the shimmering river and the swamp, which surrounded the river on both sides.

I'm going to miss dinner with Sebastian and the kids. Funny, the bizarre thoughts that go through your mind in times of crisis. Besides the voodoo ritual gone bad, the migraine, and meeting Josephine, today had been one of the best days of my life because of Sebastian. Until some idiot on steroids came along and ruined things.

The guy shoved me as though the idea of holding me that close was some horrifying ordeal. I landed hard on the blue turf, scratching my elbows, the back of my head hitting the rim of the boat.

"Asshole," I muttered through gritted teeth, rubbing the back of my head.

He frowned and said something probably equally as impressive and then tossed my backpack onto the dock, tied the boat, and reached for me.

Once we were on steady ground, I said a prayer of thanks, wanting nothing more than to just be *still* until my body adjusted to the solid surface, but Leadhead was already pulling me down the dock and giving me the first glimpse of our destination.

I stumbled.

Set back from the river, nestled in a grove of old live oaks wearing Spanish moss like the tattered clothes of long-dead ghosts, was a massive plantation house. All alone. In the middle of the swamp, set on a manicured lawn like some stubborn island that refused to sink into the sludge. The scent of river and coastal mud was thick, but tempered by the breeze off the water and the chill that came with the disappearing sun. Already frogs croaked and katydids sang.

The house had a long second-story balcony and thick white columns that seemed as stout as the oak trees on the grounds.

A few dim lights lit the tall, shutter-framed windows.

As we crossed onto the lawn, my feet sank into the soft grass as though I was stepping in sand. My mind raced with escape plans and questions, but there was no point in asking my captor anything, since he didn't seem to speak a word of English. And as we drew closer to the house, I wasn't sure if I *could* speak. The house took my breath away. Yes, it was enormous and graceful, but it seemed to bleed emotions. Sadness. Loneliness. Like a beautiful lady left alone in a sea of gray, green, and black, protected only by oak matrons in their skeleton shawls.

We crossed the first-floor porch to the front door. Inside, the area was lit by a large chandelier that hung in the foyer.

Deserted and dim. An interior designer's dream. Our wet, muddy footsteps thudded over the plank floors, straight past a grand curving staircase and toward the back of the house. He nudged me to the right, to a door that led beneath the staircase.

He spoke a few whispered words, shoving me down the rank-smelling stairwell lit with old iron lanterns. Something was very wrong with this picture. We were going *down*. Impossible in this swampy area. Granted, the house might have been built on a patch of solid ground, but even that was sinking, like everything in and around New 2.

My pulse hiked as I saw the walls, made of tightly stacked blocks of stone. Black trails of sludge leaked from the seams in places, making it look as though the stones wept black tears. The place gave me the notion that at any minute, the blocks might give way and the dark water and swamp creatures would come in and reclaim what was theirs.

I swallowed hard as we came to a long corridor. We had to be two stories under now, and the weight above us, the idea that everything around us existed on soft mud and swamp, made my blood pressure skyrocket and my palms sweat. I had to get out of here. Now. Before the claustrophobia made me panic and do something stupid.

My captor shoved me down the corridor. Lanterns lit on their own as we went, as if by magic. Then I realized in horror that we were passing cells. *Cells*. Cells with fronts of thick iron bars covered in crust and cobwebs. The interiors were black. And the smell had become suffocating. Far beyond human stench and waste to unbreathable.

My stomach turned, and I stumbled just as the guy gave a hard push to keep me moving. I fell to my knees and gagged, retching three times before he jerked me to my feet. A fine sheen of cold sweat covered my skin, and my throat burned with bile.

Four cells in, he stopped and opened one.

"No," I started in a small voice, leaning back against him, turning in his arms and clinging to him like a child. "No, please." He pulled at my fingers. Tears ran down my cheeks as we struggled, body to body, me holding on for dear life and him doing everything he could to pull me off. I was far beyond panic, mumbling words fast and shaky and desperate.

There was no fucking way I could go in there. No way. *Please, God, no!*

Finally he succeeded as my strength failed, shoving me into the cell. I fell onto my rear. The door slammed shut. There was slime on my palms, and my knees slipped in something as I crawled to the door and grabbed on to the bars, screaming after him.

"Don't leave me! Please!"

As he left, each lantern blinked out.

My nose grew stuffy. The tears continued hot and fast down my face, which I pressed against the bars, desperate to hold on to the light, to *see* the light. "Please."

And then there was nothing but velvet blackness and silence.

I cried for a long time, until there were no more tears left. My grip on the bars relaxed, and I slumped next to them, still holding on, still trying to be as close to the exit as I could, afraid of what lurked or *had* lurked in the cell.

Eventually I became as silent as the space around me. My mind settled and began to refocus. It was clear that the guy who'd brought me here was the same type of guy as the one who'd attacked me in Covington. And by killing him, I hadn't stopped the curse. A light wave of nausea rolled through my gut. Was that why I was here, to be beheaded like my grandmother? No. No, that was *not* going to happen. I squeezed my eyes closed, concentrating on the faint *drip, drip, drip* of water and the steady rhythm of breathing, which might've been from the cell next to mine or the one across the corridor.

There was a small shuffling sound. A grunt. I straightened. A shiver went down my spine and lifted the hairs on my arms and legs. There were others in these cells. I was not alone. A relief, but also another reason to worry. Friend or foe? Kidnapped like me or dangerous? I sat against the bars for what seemed like hours, thinking of Sebastian and the kids back at the house on First Street. Were they looking for me? Giving up? Turning in for the night?

A small light began to grow in the cell diagonal from mine. I rubbed my dry eyes with the back of my hand. The light reached capacity, which was only a faint glow, no brighter than a candle on its last breath.

A shadow appeared on the wall inside the cell, and it looked as though the person making it was sitting against the wall I couldn't see. "Hello?" The voice that came out of me was hoarse from screaming and almost too soft to hear. I tried again. "Hello?"

"Hello, she says," a sharp, high-pitched voice cawed from down the corridor, laughing and mimicking. "Poor baby. Poor, *poor* baby." Gleeful laughter followed, grating on my spine like nails on a chalkboard, as though a bird had been given voice. A mean bird. "Get used to it, girlie. Get used to it. Hello, she says. Hello, hello, hello . . ." More laughter, which finally subsided when another voice, also down the hall, told it to "shut the fuck up."

A few more cells began to glow. The occupants in them obviously had some source of light that I didn't.

The shadow in the diagonal cell moved and a black form, backlit by the glow, appeared at the bars. "What did you do?" said a gruff, masculine voice. Very deep, but very quiet.

"Nothing. I didn't do anything."

Voices laughed. Tears pricked my eyes again, but I blinked them back.

"You might not think so, but to Her you have."

"Her?"

He chuckled, an echoing rumble. "You must be a Beauty, then."

"A what?"

"It's the Beauties who have no idea why they're here. The ones who attracted the wrong kind of attention, took attention off Her." He sighed. "The Beauties all die so quickly...."

"I'm not a Beauty." And I'd never believe I was. I saw it in the face in the mirror, the *possibility* of beauty, if not for the freakish hair and the teal eyes that were too light. Too weird to be beautiful. "And I'm sure as hell not going to die here."

The man moved, sitting down next to the bars. "Why are you here, then?"

"I wish I knew. One minute I'm minding my own business in the French Market, and the next I'm attacked by some weirdo foreign guy who likes to carry daggers and shields."

A hiss sounded. "The French Market? In the city? New 2?"

"Yeah," I answered slowly. "What's New 2 have to do with it?"

"The Sons of Perseus," the guy said. "τέρας hunters. They are forbidden within the city. Damn it," he swore under his breath. "She has broken the compact."

"Excuse me if I'm a little lost here, but what the hell is a τέρας hunter? And what do you mean by 'compact'?"

"The compact is—was—an agreement between the Novem and Herself after the hurricanes struck. We turned over a τέρας hunter who had betrayed her in return for her promise to never breach the city again. τέρας means 'monster' in Greek. Any creature that is not human. The Sons of Perseus, they hunt them. They hunt the poor, unfortunate souls that were Made by The Bitch herself."

The bird voice laughed, and I could picture the person jumping up and down. "The Bitch! The Bitch, The Bitch, The Bitch!"

"Will you shut . . . the fuck . . . up?" came the same annoyed voice as before.

"For Her to have done this, you must be very important. Who are you?" the guy near me asked as though he hadn't even heard the commotion down the corridor.

"You first. Who's 'The Bitch'?"

Whispers. Sad, fragile whispers began, carrying down the corridor. Whispers of one word, one word that finally became something.

Athena.

The hairs on the back of my neck stood straight. The bird voice mixed with the others in a whisper that sounded like awe. "Athena."

Ten

I LAUGHED IN DISBELIEF, THE SHARP SOUND REBOUNDING DOWN the corridor, the echo eventually replaced by the flat, continuous drip of water against stone. First vampires, witches, and shape-shifters. And now this.

This is what Alice must have felt like when she tumbled down the rabbit hole.

No one moved or spoke, and I got the feeling that my newbie response had brought a sadness to the underground prison, as though everyone here was, for a moment, remembering their own first night, their own horror and disbelief.

"How long have you been in here?" I asked the figure across from me.

"Nothing brings the madness back faster than thinking

about time," he said softly. "Best to not ask that question. No one likes to dwell on it."

Oh. Right. "And Athena . . . you're talking *the* Athena, Greek goddess, hung out on Olympus?"

"She is, unfortunately for us all, very real."

My back slumped and my eyelids fluttered closed as a dumbfounded cackle bubbled to my throat and lodged there. What the hell was happening? Why the hell couldn't I get out of this freaking nightmare? *The gods were real.* I didn't know how to react, so I just sat there feeling blank and squeezing the bars as tightly as I could. And even more bizarre, I'd somehow pissed off one of the *gods*.

It figures.

I pulled my knees into my chest and hugged them, resting my head on my forearm and sighing on the words: "I can't believe this." The man across from me chuckled softly; his hearing had to be incredibly acute. I lifted my head. "They're all real, then, the gods?"

"Some are, yes. The myths we all know, the gods you learn about in school, some are mere fiction, but many of them are or were once real. And there are some never mentioned in the chronicles of mankind, who even now roam the earth. The pantheons are not what they used to be. The Age of the Gods has long passed, and now they struggle for survival just like the rest of us.

Entire families wiped out, gods overthrown, imprisoned . . . There are only two pantheons left, made up of those who survived the wars and rivalries. And Athena would like nothing better than to wipe her enemies off the face of the planet. In the meantime, she amuses herself with plots and vindictive pleasures."

"So, what did you do to piss her off?"

He laughed. "I was born to power."

Another whisper drifted from down the hall. "I'm born too."

"Me too."

"And me."

"And me."

My heart thudded harder. These people, their only crime was being born. Was that my crime as well?

The bird voice came next. "Born or Made. Born or Made. We are all Born or Made."

"Which are you?" I asked louder, pressing my face to the bars so my voice would carry down the hall.

"Made. Made. Made me, she did." It screeched, a contained, very birdlike squawk, and chills spread up my arm.

Another voice, female, came from the darkness. "Made."

I counted seven. Seven people were down here. And I was number eight. I could understand being born to power, but "Made"? "What does it mean to be Made, exactly?"

"Made from human into something . . . else. Made into τέρας.

As punishment. To fight for her. Sometimes on a simple whim. Athena is harsh, judgmental, and will not be overshadowed. Sometimes all it takes is being beautiful," the man across from me said.

The bird voice spoke again amid a ruffling of movement. "Not all of us are here because we are Born or Made. There is one here for another reason...."

"Go fuck yourself," came that irritated, deep voice from before. Male. The same accent as the two hunters who had come after me. An accent I now understood to be Greek. The bird screeched in an angry response, the sound making me cover my ears as it bounced off the stone walls.

No one spoke afterward.

I rested my head back against my forearm and closed my eyes, letting my body rest. My mind, however, raced, going over the events of the last two days that had led up to this. I couldn't be too far from New 2. This place was probably one of the many plantations that existed, or had existed, along the River Road. All I had to do was get out of this cell and back to the dock. Or to a path. I couldn't stay here, not in this darkness, not surrounded by swamp and sludge, which could implode the walls and drown me in mud—inescapable, suffocating mud.

My blood pressure rose with the thought. My fingers flexed with the desire to cause some serious damage. Damage to myself.

Damage to the cell. Didn't matter. My foot bounced my leg with the speed of a locomotive. Small way to release the adrenaline compounding in my body. Bounce your leg or slam your fist against the bars and break your hand. Seemed an easy choice, but I was thinking the pain might feel pretty good right about now.

Breathe, Ari. You've been in worse spots than this. Seven years old. Locked in a dirty dog crate for three days straight and fed dry dog food thrown through the front grate. My punishment. Foster Mom Number Two had served chicken breast for supper, completely raw in the middle. On purpose. I refused to eat it, got pinned to the floor, raw chicken shoved down my throat. Puked it right back up onto Number Two's hand as she tried to duct tape my mouth, and the rest became just another chapter in my history. Whatever. I'd handled that small space. And I sure as hell could handle this one.

I sniffed hard and wiped at my nose, eyeing the dim light down the hall, remembering other events in my past....

Don't think about it.

Instead I thought of Bruce and Casey, their easygoing nature and frequent smiles; both no-nonsense and tough, but kind and loving in their own way. I thought of Crank and Violet, and the gifts that were still in my backpack, wherever that was. And Sebastian. How my stomach went weightless whenever his image popped into my head. How much I'd liked holding his hand on the way to Café Du Monde. How kissing him had erased every single thought from my mind and, for once, just allowed me to be in the moment, completely swept away.

A cough echoed from the darkness.

I lifted my head from the bars, my knee finally done bouncing. I knew I was experiencing what everyone else here had already gone through. The panic. The disbelief. The fear.

My teeth bit down gently on my lip. And they'd all probably thought of escape too.

My fingers felt along the bars, looking for the lock. It was square with a large keyhole big enough for my pinkie, which fit to the first knuckle and then could go no more. I wiggled it, feeling for the jagged ridges.

"It won't open," Diagonal Guy said. "Our powers don't work down here."

My hand stilled. "Powers?"

One syllable came out of his mouth before the door from above opened, sending a shaft of welcome light racing down the hall. It wasn't all that bright, but when you've been in darkness for several hours, it seemed like the sun had come out. I shielded my eyes as footsteps proceeded down the steps.

"Good luck, girlie," the bird voice said.

I tensed, standing and grabbing the bars, looking hard to

the guy near me, for comfort, for help, for anything.

"He'll take you to Athena," the man said quickly. "She won't come here. It will be over before you know it."

The lanterns along the walls flickered to life, one by one, as the footsteps drew closer. The large black silhouette stopped in front of my cell. It was the same man who had put me here. A τέρας hunter. A monster hunter. And he had my backpack slung over his shoulder. He slid the key into the lock, opened the door, and reached in.

I reacted without thinking, relying on years of instinct and a seriously strong need to get the hell out of there. I grabbed his wrist, jerking him inside with all my might, knowing he wouldn't expect that. If anything, he'd assume I'd try to run, to get out, not get him *in*.

Caught off guard, he barked his surprise and stumbled inside, slipping on the grimy floor and sliding into the blackness as I snagged the bag off his shoulder.

The bird voice shrieked. Shuffling sounded. The hunter cursed loudly.

Quickly I unzipped the bag and felt for the dagger, pulling it out blade first and then flipping it so that the hilt slapped into my palm. Then I waited, heart pounding and limbs tingling with adrenaline.

My eyes were a bit more accustomed to the dark than his,

so I had the advantage. My fingers flexed. Movement. I got only a one-second glimpse of him as he surged out of the blackness. I dropped to both knees, calves and feet tucked under me, as his arms reached for where I'd once been. His feet hit my knees and he fell forward as I leaned back, so far back that my head touched the grimy floor, and at the same time, thrust up with the dagger. His hands hit the bars. He groaned.

Warm drips hit my face. The scent of iron was thick and nauseating.

His blood slid down the hilt of the dagger and onto my hands, trailing over my forearms. I stayed still, breathing heavily. Not moving. The cells went quiet. My back and stomach muscles strained as he slumped his weight onto the dagger. My arms burned, but still I didn't move. And then suddenly he twitched. Three seconds later his body transformed to smoke and disappeared into that invisible updraft. The weight was relieved from my body, and I collapsed back onto the floor.

I rolled to my side, disbelief flooding me. Quickly I wiped my bloody hands on my jeans and then shook them hard, trying to relieve myself of the trembles. It didn't help. I shoved the dagger back into the backpack, wiggled the key out of the lock, and then eased out of the cell.

The way to freedom was lit from my cell to the stairs, but I turned away from the light to face the blackness of the corridor.

Every nerve ending I had was firing, urging me to run, but I stood still, heart hammering, and said loud enough for them to hear, "I'm out."

Lights from the cells appeared again, just bright enough to reveal the hallway. I went to the cell across from mine, but it was empty. The next held the guy who had spoken to me. He was standing at the bars, waiting, his gray eyes bright with anticipation.

I gasped when I saw his face. "Oh my God."

He frowned. "What?"

"Nothing," I said, hands shaking and going to work on the lock. "You just remind me of someone."

The door popped open. He stepped out. Tall, like Sebastian, those gray eyes boring into mine. His face was covered with a shaggy black beard and his hair was long and tangled, but there was no doubt in my mind. It was like looking at Sebastian, only aged by thirty years. He urged me down the hall.

I went to each cell, unlocking and not really looking too closely at the occupants. They all looked the same. Dirty, with wild, tangled hair and ratty clothing. Only their eyes burned. With fear. Fright. With a taste of freedom, but too scared to hope just yet.

I came to the next cell, and this time stumbled back, my heart in my throat.

"Hurry!" the bird voice hissed.

I gulped and moved to the lock, hands shaking worse than before. Its claws wrapped around the bars and its sharp, curved beak was inches from my face as I worked the key. The lock popped. I glanced up into round black eyes, ringed in yellow, but in some small part I saw humanity there. Sadness. It blinked. "Made," it said quietly, almost ashamed.

I pulled the door, stumbling back as the six-and-a-half-foot-tall harpy walked out. There was no other word in my vocabulary to describe it. Humanoid, bird, and scary as hell.

Two more cells left.

I opened another cell, this one completely black. A woman with the body of a black spider from the waist down scurried out. All the blood drained from my face. "Thank you," the creature said, and gave me a nod that spoke volumes.

Holy shit.

The last cell. I kept going. I had to. It was the only thing preventing me from hysterics. *Keep going. Deal with it later.* My hands were shaking so badly now that I nearly dropped the keys. But the Sebastian look-alike placed his big hand over mine. "No. He stays."

I did a double take. "What?" The person inside had not even come to the bars. His silhouette showed him sitting back against the wall, one leg drawn up. "We can't just leave him."

"He is a τέρας hunter. Like the one you just killed. He put some of us in here. He does not leave."

A slow, icy feeling sank into the pit of my stomach. I glanced from the figure to the bearded guy, an unexplainable dread mixed with something very similar to sorrow. He was a τέρας hunter. One of Athena's grunts. Who knew what he'd done to displease her, but it felt wrong to leave him. Wrong, wrong, wrong. I shook my head.

"Hurry!" the harpy's urgent voice came from the steps.

Older Sebastian grabbed the keys from my hand and walked away. My feet seemed to grow roots. I couldn't move. I looked to the shadowed figure in the cell, feeling as though my heart was shrinking. "I—"

"Just go," came his gruff voice. It was the same voice that had told the harpy to "shut the fuck up." "I belong here."

"Girl! Come on!" came Older Sebastian's voice again.

I swallowed as hot tears cut through the dirt and grime on my face. "No one belongs in here," I said.

"Killers do. Just go. Take the trail behind the old slave quarters. It will lead to the road back to New 2. You might have enough time to hide. But it won't stop Her. She's already broken the compact with the Novem by sending her hunter into the city. And she'll send more. Don't give up your dagger. It's the reason you just gained your freedom. That blade is the only thing capable of killing a hunter. Keep it safe and secret."

I hit the bars, wanting to scream for the keys back.

"Hurry. You've little time left."

"Thank you." It sounded totally inadequate, but I said it anyway, my voice breaking. The hunter didn't respond.

I ran, feeling like I had just done something wrong, something I knew I'd always regret. I flew passed Older Sebastian and took the steps two at a time.

No one was in the house as we raced out the front door.

I took the lead, heading across the large yard and underneath the canopy of oaks to the buildings behind the main house, the three-quarters moon lighting our way.

When we rounded the corner to the restored slave quarters, I stopped, my lungs straining and chest heaving. My eyes scanned for the trail and found a small footpath that led into the swamp, a jumble of vines and palms and cypress trees.

A low, anguished cry brought my attention back to the group.

The spider woman was on her knees, all woman now, completely naked, her face thrown back to the light of the moon and her arms limp at her sides. Tears of relief and joy streamed down her face as some of the others helped her to stand.

"I have been unable to shift for two hundred years. Thank you."

I met the woman's dark eyes. She was gorgeous in a Queen of the Night kind of way, with long dark hair and sharp, seductive features. "You're welcome," I said, trying to sound normal, but it came out broken and high.

Her eyes narrowed as she took in my white hair and teal eyes. "You are τέρας?" she asked.

I opened my mouth to say no, but then hesitated. I wasn't sure how to answer, or what the hell I was doing out here in the middle of nowhere. "I don't know what I am," I finally answered.

Older Sebastian placed a soft hand on my shoulder. "You'd know if you were Made. Some who are Made, like Arachne here, have the power to shift back to human form."

"This is where I leave you all." Arachne turned back to me. "If you ever have need of me, just call my name. I will hear."

She nodded once to the others and then darted into the blackness of the swamp.

"This is where I leave you as well," the harpy said.

Its large head leaned close to me, eyes intense, beak almost touching my nose. A claw reached out, the point touching the small crescent tattoo on my cheekbone and then poking at my hair. It laughed. "Freed by a Beauty. Figures. I was like you once. Don't let Her get to you, girlie. I take my chances in the swamp." Closer, the beak grazed my cheek, sending a cold shudder down my spine. Then it whispered in a voice only for me, "Say my name out loud, and I will hear no matter the distance." It paused and whispered a name.

The magic in that word made goose bumps erupt on my skin.

The harpy unfurled her massive, leathery wings and took flight.

The force blew the leaves around my feet and stirred my hair.

She was gone.

"Let's go," Older Sebastian said, heading with quick strides to the trail.

We stayed in a pack, moving fast through the swamp. No one spoke, but the sounds of our panting and our passage through the undergrowth seemed unnaturally loud in my ears.

It felt like we traveled for hours before we came to a dirt road. Finally—no more leaves swatting at my face, no more stumbling over roots and stepping in calf-deep mud and water. We jogged down the center of the track, careful not to fall into the tire treads on either side.

Instead of getting tired like I was, the others seemed to increase speed, to get a second wind. I remembered Older Sebastian's mention of power: *Our powers don't work down here*, and I wondered if their powers—whatever those were—were returning, if that was what gave them this extra burst of energy while I was about to sit down in the dirt, call it quits, and pass the hell out.

But still I went on, concentrating on putting one foot in front of the other until my entire body was numb and hot, and my nostrils dry to the point of pain.

Dawn hadn't made it to the horizon as we got our first sight of the city lights from Uptown, making our way down Leake Avenue, to St. Charles and past Audubon Zoo.

A few of the ex-prisoners stopped. *Thank God!* I didn't question the decision, just bent down, both hands on my knees, and tried to catch my breath. The strain in my lungs, the dry burn in my throat; it was unlike anything I'd ever felt before. Then I put my hands on my hips and paced in a small circle, trying to walk it out, to calm my overworked heart.

One of the prisoners drew in a giant inhale and then shook his body like a dog shaking off water. Some of the dirt flew off him, but not much. He grabbed my hand and kissed it. "I am Hunter Deschanel. I owe you my life. Call on me, and I will return the favor if ever the need arises."

Hunter stood back. The two women in our group and another guy stepped forward, thanking me. All I could do was nod. I didn't feel like they owed me anything. The fact that I'd escaped that cell was a fluke, and I knew it. If that blade hadn't been in my backpack, we'd all still be underground.

Hunter and the rest of the group, except for Older Sebastian, fled into the predawn light, fading as they broke apart and went their separate ways.

I turned to the Sebastian look-alike, his gaze on one of the retreating shadows. Just the two of us now. In the dark, empty street.

He tipped his head back and slowly closed his eyes. His chest rose as he drew in a deep, cleansing breath. The air stirred, blowing at his clothes and hair as it wrapped around him—a gentle tornado that obscured him from view for a moment. It wiped away the dirt and replaced his rags with jeans, a crisp white shirt, and a thin black coat that reached his hips. His black hair was tied back from a clean-shaven face, just the faintest hint of stubble left on his jaw. A black tattoo swirled from somewhere beneath the left collar of his shirt, up the side of his neck and jaw to wind around his ear and temple.

Blood pounded through my veins. I swallowed and forced myself not to take a step back, my body going completely still as he turned his head in my direction. Shock stole my voice. A tremor went through me. I nodded, trying to catalog this latest scene into all the other supernatural wonders I'd witnessed in the last two days. It shouldn't surprise me, really, not after what I'd learned in Athena's prison or seen outside of it.

"I take it you have met my son."

Eleven

"SEBASTIAN IS YOUR SON." IT WASN'T REALLY A QUESTION, JUST an echoing statement. The fact was obvious. They were near identical. Same black hair, same gray eyes, same facial structure, though Sebastian's lips were a bit fuller and darker. Maybe I just needed to say it out loud, to ground the truth into reality.

"Michel Lamarliere." He held out a hand, eyes containing nothing but warmth and purpose, and deep, deep knowledge. I shook it quickly, distracted by his eyes and the slight tremor of apprehension that continued through me. His large hand made mine feel small and inconsequential. Weaker. Younger. All true, but I sure as hell didn't have to like the feeling.

"If you can just point me in the right direction to the Garden District," I said, hearing the awkward tone in my voice.

Michel released my hand, eyes narrowing over my shoulder as he assessed our position. "This way."

I let out a slow breath and fell in step beside him, heading down a street framed on either side by small shotgun-style houses.

"How is he, my son?"

I barely knew Sebastian. *You know him enough to suck face.* My eyes rolled at the asinine thought. I cleared my throat and grabbed the straps of my backpack, easing them away from my shoulders and armpits and focusing on the broken asphalt. "He seems to be doing okay. I don't really know him that well. He's helping me with something. Well, his grandmother is too. Going to help us—I mean, me."

"Josephine?"

"Yes. Is she your mother?" As soon as I asked, I remembered Sebastian saying that Josephine was his mom's mother.

"Gods, I'd never want *that* curse. No, Josephine was my wife's mother. What are they helping you with?"

"A curse," I said, deciding quickly to trust him. "My curse."

He nodded thoughtfully, linking his hands behind his back as we strolled down the desolate street. Old houses, trees, cars were all wrapped in shadows. And the dim orange lights that winked through dirty glass windows or off in the distance only accentuated the darkness.

Now that my body had cooled from the marathon run, my skin had become damp and cold. A faint shiver bloomed on the back of my neck, but it wasn't from the cold. "Why were you . . ." I hesitated, not sure how to ask.

"My only crime against Athena was being born of a certain heritage, and taking a stand against Her insanity. What is your name, child?"

"Ari." I remembered Sebastian's words. The breakdown of the nine families. The Lamarlieres were witches. The power passed through the female line. "I thought only the women could do—"

"Magic?"

I shrugged. What other word was there for what he'd just done?

"It runs through the males occasionally," he explained.

"And that makes Sebastian . . ."

"Part warlock, part vampire. And very special." Yeah, Sebastian had neglected to share that fact. "I haven't seen my son in nearly a decade," Michel said sadly, regretfully. "He must think I abandoned him, left him. I'm sure, in my absence, Josephine has made her impression. I fear her influence will have changed him."

"I don't think you have to worry about that. Sebastian plays by his own rules."

Michel grinned, pride and the shine of tears coming into his eyes. "That is good."

I nodded, letting the subject of Sebastian die out. Ten years was a long time to be separated, and I could only imagine the heavy things running through Michel's mind right now. "So why didn't the harpy turn back to human form like Arachne? That *was* a harpy, right?"

Michel let out a small chuckle. "Yes. And you, Ari, are the only one, in all the time that I have been in that sinkhole, she has given her true name to. Guard it as the gift it is. The harpy cannot turn back to her human form because Athena made her without the ability to shift. Arachne, however, was made with the means to transform, so she could lure Athena's enemies with a beautiful form, then change and strike them down."

Michel stopped walking and faced me. "You set us free and you killed a Son of Perseus. She will come after you tenfold now."

"Two, actually." I winced. "I killed two of them."

He blinked in surprise. "Then you have done something no one has ever done before." Continuing down the street once again, he said, "You must stay in the city, under the protection of the Lamarlieres. We are one of the nine, and with the power of the Novem we can keep you safe."

"Thanks, but all I really want is to have this curse lifted, and Josephine knows how to do it. Then I'm out of this nightmare. No offense."

He scratched his chin. "You must be careful of Josephine."

"I know. I've been warned. But she knew my mother, and she knows how to help me."

He stilled and began staring at me hard, his mind working, taking in my information, processing, giving me the willies because whatever conclusion he was coming to did not look good. He swore under his breath. "Eleni's daughter."

A rush of cold went through my stomach.

"No wonder you're wanted."

I didn't ask by whom. Josephine. Athena. Suddenly I didn't want to know. I just wanted to be fixed. Maybe once my curse was gone, neither one of them would care so much about me anymore.

He reached out and placed his hand on my shoulder. "Don't be afraid," he said. "This is for your own good."

I tensed. Right before the ground dropped out from beneath me and my vision went black.

Images—disjointed, random—filled my mind. The prison. Violet in her mask. Pascal's milky white nose, mouth agape, teeth showing, staring so close. Mother in front of a mirror, tears streaking down her face, hands shaking as she tried to dig imaginary snakes from her scalp. The harpy and her great wings, flapping, hitting glass and chirping with a chorus of other birds. Sunlight. Clean-smelling sheets.

Clean sheets?

My eyes popped open. Birds moved and fluttered and chirped in the vines that crawled up the side of one window. I rubbed my eyes, wiping the filmy tears that came with my yawn. My face felt old and heavy, my body wooden and tired, but as I moved and stretched and snuggled into the soft down mattress, I began to feel like my old self. The blades of the ceiling fan went slowly around, caressing me with a gentle breeze.

It didn't take long to see that I was in a ground-floor bedroom, with a view of a garden courtyard, similar to the one at Jean Solomon's house on Dumaine Street. Someone had dressed me in a white tank and a pair of white drawstring pajama pants. My feet were bare. I got off the bed and crossed over the hardwood floor to a set of French doors, opening them to a beautiful winter sunset in the French Quarter. The air was cool, but the sun had warmed the brick pavers so they emanated heat.

I'd slept the entire day, from dawn to sunset—spending all night breaking out of "goddess prison" and trudging through the swamp and back to civilization can do that to a girl.

No locks on the doors. No prison. Just put into a soft bed by Michel. Michel, who knew about my mother. Who, probably, knew all about my curse.

Beyond the tall brick walls, the clip-clop of hooves on the street and the creak of carriage wheels caught my attention.

Muffled voices drifted through the courtyard tunnel. My hand squeezed the door frame. God, I wished my mother was still here, that we'd had more time together. That she could see me now, to see what I'd grown into.

I began to see why my mother had chosen to live in this place. It was full of beauty, not only seen, but felt and heard and tasted. I drew in one more cleansing breath, trying to quell the tightening in my chest before going back into the bedroom.

A neatly folded pile of clothes had been placed on the dresser. Not my own. I figured those had been ruined beyond washing. A pair of jeans. Stretchy black T-shirt. My black boots had been cleaned, and there were new socks and underwear, too. My backpack sat on the floor next to the dresser. After a quick search, I was relieved to find it hadn't been opened. My gun, of course, was gone. That had been taken by the τέρας hunter, but the blade was there, and that was all that mattered; the blade was way more lethal than the gun.

In the en suite bathroom, I took a quick shower, washing my dirty hair twice and thinking of how I'd gotten here, what I'd do now, and how in the hell I was going to make Michel tell me everything he knew. I squeezed the water from my hair, wondering why Athena wanted me, and if it was she who had cursed my family to begin with. But why would a goddess curse us to die at twenty-one? Why make us have unchangeable hair like this and eyes the color of a neon sea? If anything, it *attracted* attention, something Michel had said Athena hated. So why?

I dried off, made use of the toiletries that had been set on the vanity, and then dressed in the new clothes. Under the sink I found a hair dryer.

My hair was still damp by the time I gave up and began braiding the large pile into something more manageable and less eye-catching. Once done, I left the room feeling energized, swinging my backpack over my shoulder and going in search of something to eat. I couldn't remember the last time I'd eaten.

Ah, yes I could. Beignets with Sebastian.

The house was enormous and filled with ancient artifacts and antiques. The lair of a warlock, for sure. On the second floor, I passed through a double parlor. Voices drifted from a set of tall wooden doors. I hid behind a large urn as a servant carried out a tray, bringing with her voices that carried my name. After the maid passed, I peeked around the urn and got a glimpse of a massive library. Checking for anyone else, I eased up, stuck out my toe, and let the door come to rest slightly ajar.

"It's too dangerous to keep her here, Michel. You know this. Athena will bring the full force of her power against us."

"Rowen is right. You saw what harboring Eleni cost us and this entire city. Those hurricanes nearly destroyed everything."

"But together we had the power to protect us. Together we are strong," Michel said. "And together we will be strong enough to shelter this child."

"Not while she carries the curse," another voice said. "Even without Athena, that child is a danger to us and everyone in this city. No power can stop what she can do once she matures."

"She has not come into her curse. She is no harm to us now. If we help her get rid of the curse," Michel proposed, "she will be of no use to Athena and no harm to us."

"Help her get rid of it?" This from Josephine. "Do you realize what an asset this girl can be to us? Think of the power we will have. Power over the gods. We can be rid of them forever."

A bang issued as something was slammed against wood. Michel's voice was harsh. "Listen to you, Josephine! This was what got us into trouble the first time. Had you not tried to use Eleni, we might not even be in this situation now. And now you will use her child? For power?"

"For protection," she snapped. "Athena has been an enemy to us since the Inquisition, when she tried to wipe all of us off the face of the planet. She is afraid, afraid of us becoming too powerful, afraid of her own creations coming back to defeat her. We keep the child and let her become what she was meant to be. Then Athena, or any god for that matter, will not dare challenge us."

"What do you suggest? Imprisoning her? No. I forbid this."

Josephine laughed. "You cannot forbid anything, Michel. This is a council. And majority rules."

"I am not comfortable using a child in this manner, but we cannot sustain another blow to the city like the one thirteen years ago," said a new voice. "We have had peace in New 2, a peace we have been seeking for ages. Harboring or helping this child will cause a war between us and Athena. I say she goes, takes her chances outside The Rim."

"No, she cannot go," Michel said. "Think about it, Nickolai. She can't hide from Athena. That girl doesn't even know what she's capable of. Once the goddess has her, she can and will use that child against us. She must stay, but not as a weapon. As a child needing protection."

My throat went dry. My heart raced. I leaned back against the wall. Blood pounded through my ears so fast that I couldn't hear any more of the conversation even if I'd tried.

I didn't know what to do, so I ran.

Out into the street, directly in front of a trotting horse pulling a carriage full of tourists. So close its warm breath fanned my cheek before I stumbled to the other side of the street.

I stopped at the corner, grabbing one of the streetlamp poles for support and gasping for air. Tears pricked my eyes but didn't spill over. I wanted to go back, to storm into that library and tell them they were all *wrong*. I was not a weapon. I didn't have powers like the Novem or the *doué*.

I'd make the decision for them. I'd leave New 2. If Athena had caused the hurricanes because the Novem had harbored my mother, then there was no telling what she'd do now because of me, and because of the hunters I'd killed and the prisoners I'd released.

Feeling wooden and empty, I walked the streets of the French Quarter as the sun went down and the streetlamps flamed to life, using the time to gather my thoughts and figure out my next move. I could find a landline to call Bruce and Casey, but the last thing I wanted was to bring them into this supernatural freak show, where I was playing the starring role.

I used my last five dollars to buy a shrimp po'boy sandwich from a small vendor in Jackson Square and then parked myself on a bench. A three-man band played jazz by the cathedral. A fire-eater performed. Light glinted off sequined costumes, masks, and beads. The place hummed with voices, with music and laughter. It was a good time to blend in, especially now that the moon was rising and the city had come alive.

Crank's painted UPS truck loomed on the curb in front of 1331 First Street, same spot as when she first brought me here to stay in the Garden District. An old Toyota Camry sat in the driveway, no tags, covered with bumper stickers. I stopped beneath the cover of an oak, hidden by the shadows of the moss that draped off its limbs. My gaze traveled across the dark street, over the iron gate, and up to the second-story windows.

The Novem had to know by now that I'd fled. But I wasn't leaving without my mother's box.

So far, I'd been able to stick to the black shadows that hung over the Garden District streets. The only light here—besides the few working ones along St. Charles Avenue—came from random houses. From my vantage point, I studied the tall house and the perimeter, softly chewing on the inside of my cheek.

Cold humidity dampened my skin. The air had become stagnant. Nothing moved. Time to go. I darted across the street, keeping my footsteps light and aiming for the corner of the wrought-iron fence. Vines had swamped this part of the fence, making it easy for me to climb over.

Once my feet landed on the soft bed of decaying leaves, I hurried to the back of the house, taking care to stay low and stick to the shadows. After a quick pause behind the edge of the magnolia tree, I darted across the patio and opened the French doors, slipping inside and shutting them quietly.

Lights were on. But the house was quiet and still. The parlor was empty, and so were the dining room "Crypt" and the kitchen. Daring to hope, I stopped by the stairs and listened. Nothing.

I hurried up the steps and made for the bedroom. If I could make it in and out without being seen, without having to explain or say good-bye . . . Maybe not the best way to do things, but it'd be easier for everyone involved.

The bedroom door was ajar, and all I had to do was push it and sneak inside. Once in, however, I stopped short.

Violet lay curled up on my/Crank's sleeping bag, facing away from me, with Pascal stretched out next to her and snuggled against the curve of her back.

My weight shifted. The floorboards creaked. Pascal raised his head and slowly turned in my direction. He blinked as Violet woke and looked over her shoulder. She pushed herself up, removing Pascal so that she wouldn't crush him, and then set him down beside her on the floor. A royal blue mask hung around her neck, and she shoved it over her face to the top of her head. She stared at me solemnly, eyes just as large and black as I remembered. A second of warmth spread across my chest, making me want to go sit down beside her, to know her, to—

No, I was leaving.

"Hey, Violet." I went to the box, aware that her round gaze followed. My hands slid around the box. *Just get the box and leave. Violet will be fine without you.* Which was a stupid thought to begin with. Violet had managed fine without me all these years, and the kid certainly wouldn't be fazed by someone she'd only known for a few days suddenly leaving.

I held the box to my chest as my throat thickened. Violet and I were the same, I realized. Different. Alone. But Violet had something I envied, something that I admired. She embraced who she was. She didn't try to hide or be something she wasn't. I, on the other hand, wanted nothing more than to be normal, to be anything *other* than what I was.

"Sebastian is looking for you. Everyone is out looking for you," Violet said in a small, even voice. I turned as she stroked Pascal's leathery back. "What happened to you, Ari?"

"Nothing." I gripped the box tighter. "Take care of yourself, Violet. Don't ever change."

I was nearly through the door when she said, "You shouldn't either, you know."

I kept walking.

Twelve

I WAS DOWN IN THE PARLOR BY THE TIME I REMEMBERED THE gifts I'd bought the day before, the day the τέρας hunter had come to the market. Quickly I set the box on the hall table and removed the puzzle for Crank, and the beignets, which were probably stale by now, for the boys. I pulled out the mask I'd bought for Violet, taking a second to rub my thumb over the soft surface and thinking I'd like nothing better than to wear a mask like that, to hide like I'd always done. A small knot of guilt formed in my gut. I wasn't exactly practicing what I preached, was I?

But then, Violet didn't have a Greek goddess after her ass or a power-hungry vamp wanting to use her as a weapon.

Suddenly the hairs on the back of my neck rose and a cold dread sliced beneath my skin.

Someone stood behind me.

My eyelids drifted closed as I drew in a deep, quiet breath, squeezing my fist at my side. Yeah. Someone was definitely behind me. And that someone was taller, bigger, and as silent as a statue. I tensed my muscles in readiness.

One. Two. Three.

Now!

I dropped down on my haunches, turning and swinging out one leg, connecting with a calf and following through until the intruder's feet lifted off the ground and his body fell back.

Funny thing was, he never hit the ground.

My fingertips braced on the floor as I drew my leg back under me, ready to pounce, but his body twisted in midair so that he faced the floor. His fingertips and the tips of his shoes hit the floor lightly like a ball, pushing him up and back to a standing position.

Completely unnatural. I wasn't dealing with a human here.

I leaped to my feet and swung, but his hand was already out to catch my forearm. The next hand came up. He caught that, too. His hard, angular face lit with arrogant victory. *Dumbass.* They always fell for that move. Now he didn't have anything protecting his groin area, his kneecaps, or his shins from my kick.

And then it clicked into place. "Daniel?" My knee froze half-bent, remembering the face and the name in the same instant.

Josephine's secretary. "What the hell are you doing here?"

There was no mistaking the fact that he'd rather be anywhere but here. With an annoyed frown, he ignored my question and released my wrists to pull out a white envelope from inside his formal black jacket. Well, no wonder he was irritated; he was here instead of at whatever ball or Mardi Gras party he'd dressed for.

He waved the envelope in front of my face. I snatched it, pulled out the card, and read over an invitation to a ball, my heart still pounding. My brow twisted in confusion until I saw the small, neatly written note at the bottom.

The Arnaud family requests your presence tonight,
12 a.m. at 716 Dauphine to join your friends
Sebastian, Jenna, Dub, and Henri.

"She has them," I whispered. My hand closed tightly around the invitation as Daniel straightened his jacket, nodded once, and then marched out the front door. *Asshole.*

Josephine Arnaud had the others. No need for the Novem to scour the city for me. All they had to do was take my friends and I would come. I wondered who else in the council knew that Josephine was holding them to get to me, if they'd made the decision unanimously.

"What does it say?" Violet asked, standing on the last stair step with Pascal. I was too angry to say, so I handed over the crumpled wad of thick paper. Violet stared at it like I'd just handed her a tennis ball. She gave it back. "I can't read."

I froze for a second, startled. Violet couldn't read? Pity stirred in my stomach. The kid had never had the chance to learn. Dub had found her living alone in a trapper's houseboat, and there weren't exactly schools and teachers living out in the swamps.

I told Violet what had been written inside the invitation, careful to keep my voice from betraying my reaction.

"What should we do?"

"I guess," I said, "we're going to a masquerade ball."

A slow, feline grin spread across Violet's face, flashing the tips of her fangs and giving me the willies. "Excellent." She dashed up the stairs and stopped halfway to turn back. "Come. Pick a costume and mask. I have lots."

I jogged up the steps and followed Violet to a room at the end of the hallway, opposite Sebastian's door. She produced a key from a black shoestring around her neck and unlocked the door. A small lamp covered in a red scarf burned near the twin bed, its four posts hung with beads and scarves and masks. It was like stepping into Mardi Gras World. Every spare inch of wall space was covered with masks. Piles of gowns and costumes had been laid flat, stacked against the walls.

The light reflected off the sequins and beads and crystals,

casting a rainbow of color on the ceiling. The effect was magical. "These are all yours?"

Violet set Pascal on the bed. "They are now. I collect these things."

"Why?"

She stared at me as though she couldn't understand the question, as though the answer was obvious. Then she began digging through piles of gorgeous creations and costumes. "The Arnaud ball is very formal. Each family has their own, and then on the last night of Mardi Gras, they have a council ball. You'll need something to blend in . . . no, not this one . . . Ah. This is the one."

Violet stood amid the pile, like a tiny dark fairy in a ring of jewels, and held a black satin gown trimmed in white. The bodice was strapless and contained hundreds of pearls and rhinestones, like stars in an inky sky. "It matches your tattoo and will look good with your hair. Like a domino. Black and white."

She stomped over the discarded gowns, handed me her selection, and then stood in front of the wall, searching for just the right mask. I really didn't care what she picked. I only wanted to get into Josephine's house and get my friends to safety. But my hands stroked the smooth fabric and my heart leaped with . . . anticipation. I suppose there was some girl in me after all, because I thought the gown was incredible.

"That one," Violet said, pointing.

I followed the direction of Violet's tiny finger to a shimmering white satin mask that tilted up at the corners and was trimmed with fuzzy little black feathers and rhinestones. It would just cover my eyes, brows, and the bridge of my nose.

I was tall enough to reach, so I lifted it down as Violet went to find her own costume. I thought about telling her to stay behind, but who was I to say that? I had no claim on Violet. The kid was her own person; she'd lived out in the swamp on her own for God knew how long. She'd do what she wanted, and it would probably offend her if I said anything to the contrary.

"Violet?" I said, removing my shirt and jeans to get into the gown.

"Hmm?"

"Are there schools in New 2?"

Her tiny shoulders shrugged, her back to me as she searched the pile. "The Novem has a school, but it's only for their kids and kids with a lot of money. Not for us. There's a woman who comes to the GD once a week to teach whoever wants to listen."

Violet emerged from the clothes in a purple dress that came to midcalf, revealing her overly large black shoes and black-and-white-striped socks. She removed the mask on her head and picked one off a dresser topped with masks. It was purple and white to match the dress, and with her black bob, the outfit actually came together in a sort of punkified way. Fairy punk, I decided.

Seeing me struggle to zip the back of the ball gown, Violet spun me around to assist. It was snug, and it shoved my breasts up, creating cleavage where I usually didn't have any. My bare shoulders and neck left me feeling a little vulnerable, but I could deal with it. The gown's hem just covered the tips of my black boots, so I left them on and then pulled the mask over my face.

I immediately liked the feeling of being hidden. Of no one knowing who I was or what was wrong with me, though the hair would give me away. I wound it into a tight bun at the nape of my neck. Violet handed over a pair of clip-on chandelier earrings made of black stones and cubic zirconia. My neck was left bare; the earrings and the mask were decoration enough.

After locating a leather belt, I strapped the τέρας blade to the outside of my upper thigh. It would smack against my leg, but the skirt was loose and flowing, so I had plenty of room to move.

"Perfect."

As we hurried down the steps, I suddenly felt as though I was living in a dream. A dream where I floated down the steps of a grand old house, a dream where I was the beauty of the ball, and the night was mine to own.

The cold air outside only added to my exhilaration as we spilled onto the empty street in a wash of color and sound. The swish of our skirts. Violet's delighted giggle. The sounds echoed all around us.

I shouldn't enjoy the swirling material around my legs so much, or the breathless excitement that came from racing down an eerie, darkened road with old, decaying mansions all around me. Peering through the mask made me a different person, a confident version of myself. It made me beautiful, mysterious, and powerful, as though I belonged to the night and to the magic that existed here like no other place on earth. And it belonged to me.

I was winded by the time we reached St. Charles Avenue, just catching the trolley full of costumed tourists. Violet paid our fare; I hadn't even thought beyond playing dress-up and rescuing our friends. At least one of us was prepared.

Talk was loud and cheerful as the car rolled toward the French Quarter, where we exited and fell into a quick stride, passing throngs of costumed people and regular folks as they made their way toward Royal Street for one of the nightly parades. Music wafted through the Quarter, mingling with revelry and clashing with the occasional tunes from clubs and bars.

The Arnaud house commanded the corner of Dauphine and Orleans Streets. It was three stories, with two balconies and lacy ironwork for railings. Ferns hung from the scrollwork and the tall windows were lit up from the inside, shadows passing by and classical music drifting from the house.

Violet and I stopped on the sidewalk opposite the house and watched as a group of masked women and men entered. Two butlers in formal attire stood sentry at the door. My hand gripped and fidgeted with the bent invitation. We'd arrived early, and in costume. And it looked like those were the only two things to our advantage. The real challenge waited inside.

"You ready?"

Violet slipped her tiny hand into mine and squeezed. She tipped her head up, her large eyes luminous even through the holes of the mask. "Yessss."

Thirteen

THE FIRST FLOOR OF THE MANSION WAS FILLED WITH MASKED people, moving through rooms, distracting me in their colorful, sparkling gowns. Pockets of conversation and laughter were carried on the occasional breeze coming through the open windows and mingled with the soft string quartet that played in the ballroom on the second floor. I went up, following the music. The ball was breathtaking and surreal, as though I'd gone to another country hundreds of years in the past.

I wove through the throng of guests to the back of the house and the balcony that overlooked the vast courtyard set with round tables, freshly cut flowers, and candle centerpieces. Waiters moved beneath glowing strands of lights hung from the tree limbs.

I gripped the wrought-iron railing and scanned the crowd

below, looking for Josephine or Michel. But it was hard to distinguish anyone in their masks. I went to relay my disappointment to Violet, but she was gone. "Violet!" I whispered, turning swiftly and going back through the house, but there was no trace of her.

The butlers had closed the entry doors and took up residence on either side. Violet was here somewhere. And so were the others. *Focus.* Josephine wouldn't hurt them, would she? Sebastian was her grandson, after all, and the others were his friends. But she herself had said she didn't have a heart.

After a complete but very discreet check of the first floor, I lifted my skirts and hurried back to the second level, intending to look there.

Dancing had begun in the ballroom. A crowd gathered to watch the spectacle of dancers whirl by in a blur of glittering colors. Slowly I made my way through to skirt the edge of the dance floor.

"Ah, a beauty among beauties," a French-accented voice said as a hand fell lightly on my arm, directing me through the onlookers. "Care to waltz?"

I opened my mouth as I was pushed gently backward. We'd broken through the crowd and were on the dance floor. His warm hand slid from my arm to my waist, guiding me toward him and spinning me around.

My body stiffened. I pulled away, his hand at the small of my back giving slightly. But he didn't release me. "I'm not the best dancer," I muttered, overcome by a deep sense of embarrassment. I didn't know how to do this. I didn't belong here. With these people. "I should really—"

"One dance. Please." He increased his steps to keep pace with the others on the floor as we whirled in one direction, in a fast and breathless oval. Sweat broke out along my back. My eyes scanned the crowd for a place to break, and— "Relax, *ma chère*. Just let me lead." My mind tried to play catch-up as he whisked me along, twirling and carrying me with the flow. "Breathe. It helps if you breathe," he said, laughter in his voice.

My exhale came immediately; I didn't realize I'd been holding my breath. My fingers flexed on his shoulder as my feet began to pick up the simple steps. We swept past a staircase, my gaze going up until the mask cut off my vision, and I was forced to pay attention to my partner. I wanted to get away, but something inside me wanted to stay, too.

His eyes, cheeks, and nose were shrouded in a simple gold mask, but he was tall and young. His lips curved in a half grin, and his eyes sparkled like two emeralds held to the light. His hair was light brown and wavy, touched by the sun, and long enough to curl over his ears and the collar of his white dress shirt. Subtle notes of cologne made me inhale deeply. *Nice.*

There was something about being behind the mask that

allowed me to relax for this one dance, to be someone else, a young woman who loved to have fun, to dance with a man, to flirt and feel special.

I whirled and whirled, losing all sense of time.

I changed partners many times, and it seemed as though each masked guy who held me grew more mysterious and handsome than the next. The music warbled. I grew drunk on it, on the beauty and the laughter and the warmness in my body.

I was let go suddenly by my partner, laughing and spinning until another caught me around the waist, my momentum slamming my front up against his chest. "Oh, sorry!" I paused, breath coming fast. "It's you again."

My first partner had returned, and he held me close, his hand warm against my back. He bent down and brushed my ear with his lips. A whoosh of light air breezed through my stomach. "Don't be sorry. I'm not." He kissed my ear and then whisked me into another dance.

"What's your name?" he asked. "Nymph? Siren? Fairy princess?"

There was something joyful in flirting, in the sense of power it gave me. "I am none of those things," I said, smiling.

"Ah, you are more, much more." He pulled me closer, our chests touching as the side of his cheek came to rest against my temple. "I shall call you the Moon Queen."

I laughed. "So what does that make you?"

"Good question." He leaned back to gaze down at me. A slow grin tugged his mouth. "Being the king would be quite boring. I'd much prefer . . . the queen's consort."

Heat seared my cheeks, and my breath became labored. His mouth skimmed my temple, slowly, lazily trailing his lips down to my cheek, my ear, and then my neck, sending hot shivers down my spine. I wanted more, wanted to fall into a careless spiral of sensations. To hell with the consequences. He pulled me closer as if sensing my need. And I let him, exposing my neck more as we spun around the room.

I swallowed, somewhere in the back of my mind knowing that it was too fast and too odd, but the mural ceiling and the lights blending into shimmering colors distracted me. His arms tightened as he kissed my neck, small, feathery kisses and hot breath that weakened my limbs. My eyes rolled, falling onto the dancers, the music fading to the background, the voices and laughter going with it.

As we floated around the ballroom floor, I saw flashes of things, wanton things. Other masked men and women, putting their lips on the necks of their partners. Some against the walls. Kissing. Sighs of pleasure. A dark-haired couple—his mouth going to her neck, her head against the wall, her eyes closed.

Around the room again. The thunder of my pulse drowned out the music. My responses became slow and lazy, but inside fire raged. As we came to the spot where the dark-haired couple kissed against the wall, I couldn't help but look again.

Oh my God—the guy's lips drew back, his teeth elongated as they sank into the girl's exposed neck. At the same moment, my partner flicked out his tongue and swirled it around my neck. My short black fingernails dug into my partner's shoulder as the girl's lips parted. I wasn't sure if I heard the moan of pleasure or just imagined it. But it rang in my ears.

My heart thudded hard, stomach flipping. I couldn't breathe. My vision grew faint and the room spun.

Suddenly the far wall pressed against my back, my partner pinning me there as his teeth grazed the skin of my neck. I was lost and didn't care. I was somebody else, a masked stranger, a desired woman.

Yes.

And then he was gone.

Cool air breezed over my hot skin. I blinked, mind hazy and unfocused, missing the contact.

"Leave her alone, Gabriel," a familiar voice said.

The drunken sensation refused to go away, but I tried my damnedest to focus, realizing that something wasn't right. My reactions were not right.

"She doesn't *want* to be left alone," my partner said. "Just ask her."

The room still spun beyond me, but the music was becoming clearer, the voices around me sharper. A figure in a plain black mask stepped into my line of sight and lifted his mask.

It was like a bucket of cold water. "Sebastian?"

Fourteen

WITH A FEW RAPID BLINKS, THE TWO GUYS IN FRONT OF ME came into sharp focus. My face became hotter than the surface of the sun as my behavior sank in and I realized what I'd almost done. *Idiot!* If I'd had one wish right then, it would've been to disappear. Just vanish in a cloud of mortified smoke.

There were blood drinkers, vampires, all around me. Taking freely from those who offered their shiny white necks, those revelers lost in some kind of hypnotic state where the only thing that mattered was sensation and need. And I would've been one of them had Sebastian not intervened.

Was I that weak, that willing to sate Gabriel's "need"?

"Ari," Sebastian said, "are you all right?"

I shoved away from the wall. "I'm fine." But I was pissed at how naive and willing I'd been, pissed at the warmth that still radiated beneath my skin and the tight confines of the gown. Thank God for the mask. At least my red face was partially hidden. I tried not to look directly at what was going on around us. The dancers still continued, the revelers still chatted, but the others, the ones embracing against the walls, in the dark corners . . . "Is this what you are, Sebastian?"

His mouth hardened.

Gabriel laughed, his eyes crinkling behind the gold mask. "Sebastian denies what he is. But he is the same as me."

Sebastian's irises went dark and stormy. A muscle ticked in his jaw. "Fuck off, Baptiste. I'll never be like you, like any of you." The resolute tone was as harsh as the hand that gripped my upper arm. "Come on, let's go."

"Even for you, Lamarliere, that's no way to treat a lady. Why don't you ask her if she even wants to go with you?"

I cleared my throat, wanting desperately to leave, to get them away from each other before something really bad happened. "Thanks for the dance," I said, signaling that I was done with our interaction.

Gabriel's expression and bearing became formal. He gave me a small bow. "It was my pleasure, Lady Moonlight," and then he stalked off.

Sebastian pulled me in the opposite direction, zigzagging through the press of bodies until we hit an empty spot near the front balcony. The fresh air coming through the open doors helped clear my head. "What the hell is going on? Where are the others? And where's Violet?"

"What's going on? What's going on is that we've been looking for you since you disappeared from the market yesterday evening, *that's* what's going on." He glared at me, nostrils flaring slightly, pulled down his mask with an angry gesture, and then marched onto the balcony.

Sebastian grabbed the iron railing with one hand and dragged his fingers through his hair with the other, letting out a long breath. His gaze fell on the street below, on the Mardi Gras revelers passing by, his profile grim from the edge of the mask down. He looked like a bird of prey, raven hair falling over the black satin mask. He wore a white dress shirt and black slacks, and the contrast of the dark mask against his pale skin made his lips seem redder than normal. Of course, anger could've been the reason for that color too.

The crass blow of a party horn from below shocked the admiration out of my mind. This place, this party, or whatever it was, had gotten to me. Had turned me into some willing plaything for a damn bloodsucker. My knuckles became white as I squeezed the railing with both hands.

"I haven't seen Violet," he said. "What the hell happened to you?"

"Long story. Your grandmother sent a note that she had Dub and Crank and Henri."

He faced me head-on, confused. "We've been searching for you nonstop until this evening, when my grandmother told me you'd be here tonight. I sent the others back home to rest."

"Your dad hasn't talked to you yet?"

He shoved the mask onto his head, staring at me as though I'd lost my mind. "My dad? My dad left when I was a little kid."

Oh hell. My anger went soft. "No, he didn't, Sebastian. He was imprisoned by Athena. He's here, in the French Quarter. I was with him earlier."

Sebastian's face went slack and very white. He swayed.

I grabbed his arm and walked him back to the long bench against the outside wall. He sat like he was on autopilot, went to rub a hand down his face, but he was shaking so badly, he gave up and just sat there in shock.

I wasn't good at this sort of thing, helping people deal with the past. I couldn't even deal with my own. Sebastian leaned forward, elbows on his knees and head bowed. I stayed next to him, unsure of what to do or say. I lifted my mask.

His head turned, gray eyes glassy. Hopeful, yet uncertain. "Are you sure it's him?"

"Yeah. You look just like him." I fiddled with the mask in my hand for a moment, wanting to help, just not knowing how. "He didn't walk out on you. I saw the prison myself."

"Fuck," he murmured in disbelief. "Where is he now?"

"He was at a house in the Quarter. I left there earlier when I heard—"

"Heard what?"

I swallowed. "That your grandmother doesn't want me to leave New 2. She thinks I'm some sort of weapon, and wants to use me to protect the Novem against Athena. But I'm not like you all. I don't have powers or the ability to stand up to a goddess."

"That's the second time you've said that name. You are talking about *the* Athena, the goddess?"

"Yeah. Screwed up, isn't it?" I said with a small smile. "Your grandmother hid my mother from Athena. It pissed Athena off, and she caused the hurricanes thirteen years ago. Now she knows I'm here and she's looking for me. From what I heard, sounds like she wants to use me too, just like the Novem."

He shook his head and let out a large sigh. "Jesus. And you don't know why?"

"No, not a clue." I drifted into silence before finally asking the question that lurked in the back of my mind. "I know what you said yesterday at the tea shop. . . ." But Sebastian could've been lying, or afraid to tell me the truth. Hesitantly, I glanced over and met his gray eyes. "Was Gabriel telling the truth? Are you really like him?"

"Gabriel Baptiste can go to hell. He likes to think I'll turn out like him." A deep, frustrated groan rumbled in Sebastian's throat. "Honestly, I might go my whole life without blood, or one day I'll start craving and needing it just like they do. Who the hell knows?"

Images of what I'd seen and felt in the ballroom flashed through my head, made more intense by the idea that Sebastian might, one day, be among the revelers. What would it feel like to be held in his arms the way Gabriel had held me?

Stupid, stupid thought, Ari.

"He shouldn't have taken advantage of you like that."

I straightened. "He didn't take advantage." *He didn't have to, because you offered yourself on a silver platter.* "I need to get out of here. I'm pretty sure your grandmother won't let me go if she finds me."

"You came for the others?"

"Yeah, but obviously she lied about that to get me here. Should've known." I glanced around, hoping to see Violet.

Sebastian stood and grabbed my hand. "Come on, follow me."

I let him guide me through the crowd, keeping my eyes straight ahead and not falling into the temptation of the vampire ball. But I was unable to resist the lure of his hand wrapped tightly in mine. It felt good and safe, even though I knew what he was, or what he was capable of.

Sebastian led me downstairs to the courtyard. The crowd was thinner outside, but we still had to weave our way around groups and tables and servers to get to the small, two-story guest house in the back.

An art studio/apartment, to be exact.

The light from the courtyard spilled into the room as we entered, revealing easels, canvases, paint supplies, and a long counter and sink. Beyond the front room were a seating area, a bedroom, and a kitchen.

"This will be a safe place to talk."

I stopped just inside the door and removed my mask. "Since when do guys want to talk?"

He paused when he realized I wasn't following him. He came back, grabbed my hand, and led me to the couch. "Look, if my grandmother wants you to stay in New 2, and there's a goddess after your ass, then yeah, I want to talk. Start from the beginning."

My skirt billowed around me as I sat down. I held the mask in my lap. It winked as one of the rhinestones caught the light from outside. I drew in a deep breath, shifting so that I could draw one leg up and face Sebastian. And then I told him everything I knew. From my visit to Rocquemore House, to the letters in the box, my curse, the guys I'd killed, the plantation house on River Road, and everything I'd learned from eavesdropping at Michel's. The words should've sounded far-fetched and ridiculous, but they weren't. They were my life. And as I spoke, it was as if the words solidified. No more disbelieving. No more thinking any of this was insane. No more hiding. Like Violet, I was different. And here in New 2, in front of Sebastian, I didn't have to pretend.

"It doesn't make sense," he finally said after I finished. "Why would Athena curse the women in your family to have eyes like yours and hair . . . like moonlight?" He reached behind my head and undid my bun, but I grabbed his hand.

"No. Please."

He continued to unravel my hair. I held my breath. A dry lump rose in my throat, and my heart began to thump harder and faster. "Why," he began in a low voice, "give your ancestors this beauty and then make them die before their twenty-first birthday?"

"I don't know." I looked down at my hands resting in my lap and shivered in the chilly air, thinking of the harpy. "I'm not sure I want to find out."

He released my hair, took both of my hands in his, and warmed them with his own. "We need to stay off the radar long enough to figure out your past."

"Too bad we can't just ask the Novem. They seem to know all about it."

I paused, listening to the hum of the party outside, the occasional burst of laughter, the clink of silverware, the orchestra. To most of the people here, it was probably a cheerful sound, but not to me. To me the sounds were deceptive and only highlighted the threat existing here. "Where do you think the others are, then?" I asked. "Because they weren't back at the house. Violet was the only one there."

"I don't know. When my grandmother's runner found us looking for you down by the river, Henri said they'd go back to the GD. I came here to clean up and wait for you."

"What about your dad?"

"If he's back, he'll be here tonight. But first we need to make sure Josephine didn't have someone pick up the others once I left. She's lost her mind if she thinks she can hold you here against your will, or use my friends as bait." He glanced at his watch and stood. "We have enough time."

I rose with him, hiking up the strap to the τέρας blade under the material of my skirt. "Time for what?"

His eyes darted away. Instantly his posture was stiff and his body language uncomfortable. "The ball gets a little crazy around midnight."

My heart skipped. "What do you mean, *crazy*?" I asked, even though I was pretty sure I knew what he meant.

"'Tis the season," he said. "The time to . . . indulge. Once

Mardi Gras is over and Lent begins, we fast too. It's tradition. So during Mardi Gras . . ."

They gorge themselves on blood, and probably sex and any number of decadent pleasures. I understood. He didn't need to spell it out. I suddenly felt very small standing before him. "So you've really never had the urge? Not even once?"

"I never said I didn't have the urge. I don't want blood to rule my life like it does some. Once you take it, it's like a drug." He stared out the window to the masked revelers in the courtyard. "Warm, rich, never enough."

I nodded, fidgeting with my mask. "Kind of like chocolate." I tried to hold in my grin. Casey always said I had a weird sense of humor that came at the oddest times.

He blinked before bursting into laughter. He had the nicest laugh and the most incredible smile I'd ever seen. It lit his gray eyes and sliced attractive little dimples into his cheeks. "Yeah. I guess it is like chocolate."

Some of the tension left the room.

He grabbed my hand and opened the door as I slid the mask over my face. "Just stay close and you'll be fine. We'll find Violet, make sure the others aren't really here somewhere, and then you're getting the hell away from this house."

Fifteen

As Sebastian led the way through the crowd, it was impossible for me to keep my eyes on his back; the lure of sequins and satin, masks and mystery, was too hard to avoid. The soft murmur of voices, the music, the colors, and the light reflecting off everything made the entire house pulse.

He moved fast, weaving through bodies, allowing me to catch only small glimpses of things, things I tried *not* to search out, but couldn't resist. I was drawn so easily, finding dark, hidden places, couples engaged in more than just dancing or conversing. My heart leaped at the flash of small, white fangs, the single drop of blood that gleamed on the corner of a smiling mouth with the same luster as a teardrop ruby, before a tongue darted out and licked it away.

Sebastian tugged at me, the movement drawing my attention. We'd stopped near the second-story balcony. The air was even cooler than before, easier to breathe, and it sure as hell helped to clear my head again.

The loud bang of cymbals and drums from outside drew closer, drowning out the orchestra. The guests inside the house surged to the balcony. Sebastian cursed, squeezing my hand tightly as we were carried with the tide and jostled onto the balcony railing as the Mardi Gras parade rounded the corner.

All around us, the guests yelled and cheered, their drinks sloshing over their glasses, their eyes lit with alcohol, their cheeks flushed with blood, excitement, and the sensory delights of the parade.

Floats began to pass by, one after another in slow succession, each depicting life at sea in some way or another. "The Poseidon Parade," Sebastian said.

Men stood aboard what appeared to be a centuries-old warship, their faces turned toward the balcony, eyes subdued beneath plain gold masks with hooked noses. They wore Napoleon-style hats and long, decorative coats and white stockings. Some of the crowd called down to them, but they didn't move a muscle, just continued to stare at us. The effect was unnerving.

Mermaids occupied the next float. They tossed beads into the crowd lining the street and up to the balcony. The people behind us pushed forward, pinning us even harder against the railing. Sebastian's arms went around my waist, and I knew it was an instinctive gesture—not because he wanted to hold me that closely.

He leaned down, lips close to my ear so I could hear. "We should check the house while everyone's distracted."

As he spoke, another float passed by, a scene depicting a sea cliff where half-naked sirens reclined, waiting for unsuspecting sailors to approach. The music that came from the float was designed to sound like a lure, a siren's call.

Suddenly gleaming flashes—bronze, glittering bodies—darted through the onlookers below. Delighted squeals burst from the crowd. Men in nothing but loincloths and bronze masks jumped onto the sirens' float. They crouched down, waiting. And then the sirens gestured with sultry, secretive smiles. The masked men approached, crawling up each siren's body and covering them with their own. The crowd cheered.

My face was on fire. My senses had gone totally haywire. I couldn't take any more. It was like that sound below had a real hypnotic effect. But it couldn't be . . . could it? This entire party was one big high. I'd gotten drunk on the sights and sounds like some lightweight, and now it was making me ill. I squeezed my eyelids closed tightly, forcing my mind to block out the distractions. I needed to get the hell out of here. Check the house. Find Violet and the others and leave.

Sebastian shifted, his thigh pressing against mine and causing the blade to move against my skin. The metal had warmed, matching my body temperature, and the strap was snug, almost too snug. But it was enough of a reminder that it sharpened my focus.

Strands of beads and candies flew over our heads. I shifted, angling away from the rail with Sebastian and allowing others to take our place. We drifted back, pulled like a wave retreating into the sea. Back into Josephine's house.

God, I needed to get out of this gown! It had become way too hot, too constricting. I removed my mask and then dug my fingers into the edge of the bodice, pulling it up and away from my skin, trying to let the cooler air in. Didn't help.

"Come on," Sebastian said, striding through the now empty room.

We hurried across the empty ballroom floor.

A French door slammed closed.

Then another. And another.

I slid to a stop on the deserted dance floor, turning to see each door close and lock all by itself. The orchestra stopped playing. Some guests, I saw through the glass panes of the doors, tried to get back in but couldn't. All around them doors slammed and locks clicked.

And then there was silence.

There was one more door open.

We watched it, waiting for it to close, but something told me it was waiting. A warning slithered down my back.

The sheer white curtains on either side of the door billowed. The air between wobbled and shimmered.

And then a tall figure stepped out of thin air.

The blood froze in my veins.

There was no doubt in my mind who strode into the room. How could there be?

The door slammed shut behind her, making me flinch.

Six feet tall. Perfect body. Wrapped from neck to wrists to ankles in thin, skintight leather, the color of dark, muted olive. There were lines in the leather, lines that looked reptilian—that looked like it had once been a living thing.

Athena.

She had porcelain white skin, emerald eyes lit from within, and long, wavy black hair that brushed her lower back. All through the strands were braids, braids woven with thin strips of leather, sinew, and bone beads—braids that looked like they'd been in her hair for hundreds of years. Tiny symbols were etched into the skin along both temples, just at her hairline.

Full wine-red lips curved up. "Not thinking of leaving, were you?" came a throaty female voice ringing with an undeniable vibration of power.

My eyes traveled over her. In shock. Couldn't speak.

"I've wondered at your existence for years, child."

I forced down a dry swallow, my feet rooted to the spot, as the goddess strode closer, a grin stuck on her face, a malicious, victorious grin. My hand gripped Sebastian's tightly.

Oh God.

My stomach rolled as the leather bodysuit Athena wore became clearer. It *moved*. It fucking moved. Like a living thing wrapped around her body, a thing that had a very faint outline of a huge face, squashed flat, as though the skin had been peeled off the bone and pressed thin, sewn together to make this . . . thing.

"You like?" she asked, a glint of delight in her eyes. "I made this from the skin of Typhon. Just a small piece of flesh, really. He was a Titan, after all."

It was obvious why Athena had chosen to wear the suit. Scare tactic. Intimidation.

Her gaze covered me from head to toe, her expression becoming nonchalant but strained, as though she was trying too hard to show she didn't care. "Not as pretty as the first one of you, but I see you have the hair and eyes."

"I don't *want* the hair or the eyes," I croaked, having to force out the words. "You can take them."

Athena's eyes crinkled at the corners, and she laughed. "Be

careful what you say, child, lest I take you literally. I did not give you the hair and eyes. Those are yours naturally."

"But—" *Then what the hell did she give me?*

"Athena, you have no rights here!" Josephine barked in a furious voice, making me jump. The door she'd burst through slammed against the wall. The matriarch of the Arnaud family marched her begowned self across the floor like the queen of England. "You have broken the compact."

"Oh, fuck your stupid little compact, vampire."

"You agreed never to set foot in New Orleans again. That was the sole reason we turned the τέρας hunter in our possession over to you. That was the deal."

"The child changes everything, Josephine. You know that. You know I cannot leave her in *your* hands. What will you do, hmm? Protect her like you did her parents? Betray her, too?"

My gaze whipped to Josephine. "You said you helped my mother."

Josephine cast an impatient look my way. "Your mother was young and stupid and didn't know what was best for her."

The other heads of council came into the room, spreading out to encircle us. The single door they'd filed through shut behind them and locked by itself. A glance over my shoulder revealed that the partygoers on the balcony were still engaged in watching the parade, though a few rattled the doors, trying to get back inside. Apparently, the Novem also wanted this to be a private affair.

Michel gave me a grave nod, his eyes telling me he was on my side, though I couldn't trust that. How could I trust anything after what I'd heard earlier?

Sebastian stiffened, and his hand tightened around mine as he saw his father for the first time in almost ten years. I squeezed back and then let my hand go slack, signaling him to go to his father, but he remained by my side.

"Enough of this, the child is one of mine." Impatiently, Athena reached out and grabbed my arm.

Fear rushed into my open mouth with a gasp, coursing down my throat and into my lungs. Athena's touch was cold, her fingers like ice as she gripped the bare skin of my upper arm.

Sebastian refused to release my hand. Athena leveled her gaze on him as the council encircled us and raised their arms straight out to their sides. The air in the room went electric as a shimmering blue line of energy connected them from fingertip to fingertip, making the circle whole.

"We forced you out before, Athena," Josephine said, her voice strong and never wavering. "And we can do it again."

Athena's thick fingernails dug into my skin, burning, signaling that soon the skin would break and blood would flow. The goddess slowly turned her attention to Josephine, her entire being going still and deadly, her voice coming out low and with more power than before. "Go ahead. Link your powers. Let them loose on me and watch your party end in a sea of blood."

I stared in horror as Josephine actually considered those words. I knew then that Josephine wouldn't give a damn if everyone here died as long as it meant getting what she wanted.

The skin-suit moved again along Athena's arm and wrist, so close to me that it made me jerk against the goddess's iron grip. Panic weaved its way in. "Why do you want me?" I burst out, pulling against her.

Athena stilled, withdrew her attention from Josephine, and then leaned down, her face inches from mine. Then she let me see what the goddess of war was really made of.

The perfect face changed from beauty to the darkest, most horrifying hell I'd ever seen. Death. War. Bones. Her face transformed into the queen of it all. Part skeletal. One eye gone, one vibrant emerald eye still intact. Bugs scurried through the space between Athena's eye socket and eyeball. Tendons pulled her lips into a smile. And inside her skull, between the ragged hair, bone, and rotting flesh, I saw movement. All through the goddess, all through her body, beneath her ribs, were the souls of warriors, the hell they'd found inside her.

Athena straightened, once again a beauty, and smirked. "We let the child decide."

I had glimpsed into the heart of war and death, and knew the goddess had the power to wipe out the entire city if she wanted. Sure there might be politics and compacts and laws that maybe even Athena was bound to, but in this, she'd ravage the world to have her prize. Me.

"No," Sebastian said, realizing which way I was leaning. He tightened his grip, but I pulled my hand from his.

"One day, Athena," Michel said, eyes on the goddess, "the creatures you made will turn on you. And the gods help you when they do."

Her head whipped around. She snarled. "And every time they try, they fail. I can put you right back where you were, Lamarliere, so shut the fuck up."

He'd hit a nerve.

My mind raced. Goose bumps rose on my skin. I thought of the harpy and Arachne, but I was too afraid to call them, too afraid of what Athena would do.

"Thirteen years ago, you nearly succeeded in your quest to destroy us," Michel said in an even voice, but his eyes were bright with hatred. "Tell me, Athena, do you regret summoning the wind and the sea? Regret your lust for power?"

"I regret nothing," she hissed.

"Oh, surely you must. Your hurricanes grew uncontrollable. Maybe if you hadn't been so *overzealous*, you could have held on to the Aegis and not dropped it into the sea."

Athena's intake of breath told me Michel had revealed something he shouldn't have known. But Michel only grinned. "There's not much to do in prison other than talk. . . . If your father, the great Zeus, were alive today and knew you'd lost his Aegis, one of his most powerful weapons, the one you *killed* him for, I bet the irony would amuse him, no? Without the Aegis you're no longer invincible."

Athena stiffened, her eyes narrowing in on Michel. Then she yanked me hard, pulling me closer. "Aegis or not, I am still more powerful than you. And this little shit"—she flicked my hair—"will be my new Aegis. I'll remove her head from her body, flay the skin from her bones, and with it make a new shield, a better Aegis than the one before. Or perhaps I will make my next Aegis a breastplate or a cape." She ran a finger down the side of my face. "Skin has many uses."

Josephine laughed. "I think you're forgetting, Athena. You killed the only god capable of crafting you a new Aegis. Losing your mind along with your wisdom, perhaps?"

Oh shit. My eyelids fluttered. Not only did Michel have a death wish, but so did Josephine. Her words made Athena's fingernails dig deeper into my skin and pierce the flesh. The sting shocked me, but just for a second. Blood streamed in a slow, thin line down my forearm.

Athena's anger mushroomed. A suffocating, heavy energy enveloped us. "I don't need to wait to use her now. I think I shall like seeing you die first, Josephine."

"You cannot use the girl," Josephine countered. "She hasn't reached maturity."

Athena's cruel mouth quirked. "Well, how about I speed up that process?" She shoved her palm against my chest.

"NO!" Josephine lunged, breaking the circle. Athena flung out her other hand, sending Josephine flying back into the wall. Sebastian appeared behind Athena.

Michel shouted, "Sebastian, don't!"

Sebastian's arm went around Athena's neck. A headlock. He squeezed hard, but her flesh gave way just long enough for his arm to pass through. He fell backward, with nothing to hold on to.

Heat spread beneath the goddess's palm, seeping into my chest, through my body and into my head. The same astounding pain I'd had in the street engulfed me, burning my brain, enlarging the blood vessels that ran under my scalp and making them throb and stretch. A screech erupted from deep within my core, rising, until it burst from my mouth. It didn't sound human.

Just as my eyes drifted closed, I saw Michel holding Sebastian back from attacking again and Josephine standing to realign the circle. The council members began chanting, the line of power among them thickening. But it didn't matter. I was dying. My head was going to explode, or implode, or melt.

I never knew I could scream so hard, so loud, or for so long, as though the sound was fed from the pit of my soul.

I saw flashes, then, in my mind. A beautiful woman who looked like me. Kind. Loving. Devoted. In a temple, a temple by the sea. A baby crying. So much death. Through the ages. Misery.

It had to stop. It had to stop. *God!* I didn't want to die!

I grabbed Athena's wrist with my right hand and clamped down hard, trying to pull her palm away and end the agony.

Anger suddenly came to the surface, for a brief second blocking out the pain in my head. My chest swelled with it. All those images, all that death, all that hurt on my family because of Athena. I'd done nothing wrong, none of us had.

I opened my hot eyes.

My hand squeezed so hard, with every ounce of strength I had. My eyes locked with Athena's. "I . . . *hate* . . . you," I hissed, wanting to get it out before I died. "For all that you have done to them . . . for being an evil . . . fucking . . . *bitch*!"

Athena flinched, eyes widening for a fraction of a second. Just a small flicker of pain and a jerk to her arm. My jaw tightened. She pressed harder against my chest, but I was somehow pulling her hand away.

I glanced down at my hand wrapped around the goddess's wrist, where Athena's white skin was turning hard and gray.

What the hell?

Both shocked, we let go at the same time.

But I took the advantage. I was good at shoving things aside and saving them for later. All that mattered now was the fight. I balled my fist and gave a swing that would've made Bruce proud. My fist connected with Athena's jaw, sending her head snapping sideways.

My heart pounded. The pain inside my head made my vision waver. I couldn't feel my knees and wasn't exactly sure how I was still standing, but I put both hands up, ready for a comeback.

Slowly Athena's hand went to her jaw. Astonishment swam in her emerald eyes, and I swear I saw a glimpse of vulnerability and embarrassment. I took a wild guess and decided that no one had ever slugged the goddess of war before.

And then she was gone.

Just like that. There one second, gone the next.

My legs gave out and I dropped to my rear on the dance floor, the gown billowing around me, making me feel very small and very much like the child everyone called me. A child pretending to be a big girl in her frilly ball gown. A child who didn't know anything about the world she found herself in. A child compared to the old and ancient beings I'd come to know.

Michel released Sebastian. He ran over, skidding down to his knees. "Ari. Are you okay?"

Numb, I could only nod.

Josephine marched forward, her heels clicking on the floor, and yanked me up by the arm. "Get up. We have work to do."

"Josephine," Michel's low voice boomed. "That is not the way to treat the person who just saved this entire house from annihilation."

She opened her mouth to argue, but the other members had moved closer too, obviously not happy with her treatment of me. She dropped my arm. "Fine." She turned to them. "Athena has gone back to lick her wounds, but this is only the beginning. She *will* wage war over this child." She lifted her skirts and swished away, yelling at the maids to unlock the doors and motioning for the stunned orchestra to begin their music again.

"Josephine is right." Michel offered Sebastian a hand to help him off the floor.

I brushed off my skirts as Sebastian rose, standing across from his father, a father he hadn't seen in years. He glanced from his father's face to their linked hands. Emotion swam in his gray eyes, and he suddenly looked like a child as well. Michel pulled him into an enormous hug.

I left them alone, watching as the guests came back into the room. The orchestra began playing, and a line of waiters came in carrying trays of hors d'oeuvres and champagne.

But the one person I noticed above all others was Violet, gliding across the floor with a spring in her step, the purple skirt flouncing, her mask down. She came right up to me, lifted the mask, and said, "What'd I miss?"

The absurdity of what had just happened finally took its toll. I laughed. I couldn't stop it once I'd started. Violet just stared up at me with her usual stoic eyes. Then she said, "I'm tired. Let's go home."

I blinked, the laughter fading.

Home.

The threat of tears stung my eyes. I opened my hand. Violet slid her tiny hand in. "Yeah. Let's go home."

Screw the council. We were leaving.

We strolled out of the ballroom and away from Josephine's call to come back.

Athena wouldn't lick her wounds forever. I knew that. But right now, I needed to go back to the old house in the GD and try to be normal for a little while, even if it was just for the night.

"Hey! Wait up!" Sebastian caught us as we exited the house. I stopped in the middle of the street. The parade was over, but people still hung out in groups, still not ready to end the party.

Sebastian looked happy for the first time since I'd met him, like the dark cloud constantly hovering above him had lifted.

"You're not staying with your dad?"

"I don't want you going back to the GD alone." His face colored slightly, and he shoved his hands into his pants pockets. "If there wasn't a goddess after your ass and bent on destroying the Novem, then, yeah, I'd stay with him for a while and catch up."

"She's not alone, Bastian," Violet said, offended.

Sebastian smiled. "I know, Violet. But the more protectors Ari has the better." He met my gaze. "My dad wants you to consider staying with him. It's safer at his house."

I knew where I wanted to be. "I'll think about it. Right now, I want to get out of this dress and eat. I'm starving. And the first places Athena will look for me are the Novem's houses, not some run-down place in the GD."

Sebastian nodded. He made a flourish with his hand. "Shall we, ladies?"

A funny feeling swept through my chest. He'd chosen me. He *cared*. Yeah, the world as I knew it was basically falling down around me and my life was in the balance, but the happiness I felt in that moment erased it all. We walked down the sidewalk, heading for the streetcar that would take us home.

Sixteen

WE FOUND DUB, HENRI, AND CRANK IN THE PARLOR, SEATED on the floor around the coffee table playing poker with a pot consisting of coins, gold teeth, cameos, and an assortment of old jewelry. There was a container of gumbo and used bowls on the table. It smelled awesome.

"Where the hell have you guys been?" Sebastian asked tiredly, plopping onto the couch and stretching his legs.

"You went to a ball!" Crank tossed her cards on the table, eyes devouring the gorgeous black-and-white gown as I parked my butt on the arm of the couch, wincing as the belt around my thigh rubbed the sore spot on my skin. Dub cast an odd look at Crank, and immediately she went indifferent. "Looks like it itches."

"It does." I wished I could've stripped the dress off right then, but I was too damned tired to make it upstairs. One thing I *could* do was relieve myself of the blade. Standing, I angled my thigh away from the others, lifted the skirt, and removed the blade, setting it and the annoying strap on the side table.

When I turned back, it was to see all eyes on me. "What?"

Dub's pale eyes went from the blade to me. "I really like her."

Crank grinned. "I vote we keep her."

Henri tossed a card facedown on the table. "Yeah," he said on a sigh. "She does fit in with the rest of you weirdos."

"Oh. Ha-ha," Crank said, dealing him a card. "So what ball?"

"Arnaud Ball," Violet answered in a singsong voice, skipping out of the room. Her footsteps echoed on the stairs.

Sebastian let out a long exhale and dragged his fingers through his hair. "What about you? I thought you guys were coming back to the house after I left."

"We decided to do a little ransacking along the way." Dub nodded to the pile of treasure on the table. "Whoever wins the pot gets to sell it to Spits."

I pulled off my boots. "Who's Spits?"

"Antique dealer in the Quarter," Sebastian answered as Violet returned with Pascal, passing the parlor to let him out back.

"You want in?" Dub asked me and Sebastian.

"No," I said, "but I want some of that gumbo."

"Help yourself." Henri gestured to the pot. "Ms. Morgan brought it by, and *petits bébés* here went apeshit over the stuff." Crank kicked him. "Ow, that hurt."

"Then stop calling us babies. And you went nuts over it too. Just like always."

"No," Dub said, "Henri went nuts over Ms. Morgan. He's in *loooooove* with her."

Henri colored fiercely, picked up a molar with a gold filling, and pinged Dub in the forehead with it. "I don't love her, you idiot."

Dub and Crank erupted into giggles as Sebastian filled two bowls. I slid onto the couch cushion and arranged my gown, pulling my feet under me. "Ms. Morgan," he said, handing me a bowl, "is like a traveling teacher, comes through the GD once a week and brings food."

"Yeah, Violet was telling me about her."

I was so hungry I ate way too fast. But damn, it was good. And filling. The poker game continued. It didn't take long for Crank to win the pot, with enough gloating to make a pro wrestler proud.

After learning the truth from Sebastian earlier—that Crank wasn't really his sister—I watched her more closely, feeling sorry for what she'd been through. Poor kid.

I thought I knew a lot about New 2, but after coming here

and spending the last couple nights, I realized I'd never had a clue what this place was really like. Besides all the supernatural stuff, I never thought there might be kids left to survive on their own, living in abandoned houses, making do in whatever ways they could.

And they were an amazing bunch of kids. I was proud to be here with them.

One by one, they went upstairs to bed, leaving me, Sebastian, and Henri.

Henri rested his back against the chair opposite the couch. "So is one of you gonna tell me what really happened tonight?"

The small lamp on the end table flickered, making the long shadows on the wall sway back and forth. The light made Henri's eyes glow—a preternatural glow that reminded me of the watchful gaze of a jungle predator.

With my nod, Sebastian told Henri everything that had happened at the ball, leaving out my dance with Gabriel and our conversation in the courtyard guest house.

"So Athena caused the hurricanes," Henri said, shaking his head.

"Who knows? She might've just made them worse, or caused the final one. Still"—Sebastian shifted his gaze to me—"none of it explains what your mom had to do with it."

"I think Athena wanted my mom like she wants me."

"Yeah, wanted you alive. Otherwise, she would've just killed you at the ball."

"And you have no idea why a goddess of freaking *war* and the Novem would fight over you?" Henri asked. I shrugged. "So what now? She'll come back for you. *Here.* Eventually she'll realize you're not with the Novem, and she'll come *here.*"

With Dub, Crank, and Violet at risk. Henri didn't need to say it aloud. I knew my presence here was a danger to them all.

A lump thickened my throat. "I'll leave."

Sebastian's face screwed into a frown. "Outside The Rim she has full power. You leave and she'll know the minute you do. You'd never have a chance. At least here the Novem has their wards on the city. Not enough to keep her out, but their power weakens hers."

"Thanks for the vote of confidence."

"She's afraid of you." He ignored my sarcasm. "I can feel it, sense it from her. It's because of your curse . . . whatever she did to your family can hurt her somehow."

I thought of Athena's wrist, the way my hand on her skin had made it harden.

Henri got to his feet, stretched his arms over his head, and yawned. "Yeah, well, a lot of good that does us if we don't even know what the curse is."

I studied Henri for a long time. The grandfather clock ticked loud in the silence. "There is one way to find out," I said, my attention shifting from Henri to Sebastian.

"Alice Cromley," Sebastian said.

Henri froze, eyes going round. "Oh, hell no! I am *not* helping you with that freak of nature, Bastian. Not again."

"You know where she is?" I straightened my posture, eyes on Sebastian. "That's what Jean Solomon meant. You've used her bones before."

"Years ago," he acknowledged in a low voice. "We found her in Lafayette Cemetery."

"Yeah, so he could learn the truth about—"

"Doesn't matter," Sebastian interrupted, becoming more certain with each word he spoke. "We know where she is. I know how to perform the ritual. Ari will see the truth, and then maybe we'll have a fighting chance."

Against a goddess of war? I almost laughed.

"We'll leave before dawn," he said, his gaze daring Henri to say otherwise.

For a moment, I thought the tall redhead would argue, but he finally nodded and walked out of the room, mumbling about getting some sleep since dawn was only a few hours away.

Once he was gone, I asked, "Why dawn?"

"Because rituals always work better at the transitions between day and night, night and day."

"Oh."

The electricity flickered again. I scanned the corners of the large parlor, feeling as though we were on a tiny island in a sea of dark indoor space, totally isolated from the rest of the world.

Sebastian broke the quiet. "You should get some sleep."

My thoughts went back to Gabonna's, where I'd slept against him, where I'd woken to a warm, safe place. Heat crept up my neck. "Don't think I can sleep right now."

"Yeah, me neither."

The silence should've been awkward, but it wasn't. I drew in a deep breath and snuggled deeper into the couch cushions, resting my head against my arm, which lay draped along the armrest. No need for words. Neither one of us wanted to go upstairs, to separate, to try and sleep. A nap was all we could afford right now, if I could even manage that.

Sebastian shifted, getting comfortable, lifting his legs to rest them on the coffee table and leaning back with his arms crossed over his chest, eyes closing. I watched him for a while, trying to relax, trying to stop the whirlwind of thoughts coursing through my mind, jumping from event to event, repeating the last few days over and over, all the things I should've done, all the things I wished would've happened.

The τέρας hunter, the one I'd left behind in the prison, kept coming back so vividly that I could smell the stench and the

mud. And his voice. The bitterness. The brief moment of kindness when he told me the quickest path to freedom. But why?
Why would he care? And why was he in there to begin with,
besides obviously pissing off Athena?

The fact that we'd left him behind burned sour in my gut. A
mistake, no matter what Michel and the others thought.

Alice Cromley's bones held the key to everything. If I
understood the power I held over the goddess, the reason she
wanted me so badly, maybe it would be enough to guarantee
my safety and keep Athena out of New 2 for good. And maybe,
once all was said and done, I'd be able to return to the plantation house and set the hunter free.

Sebastian's breathing deepened.

Funny how he could fall asleep so fast despite the situation.
Bruce was the same way. He could fall asleep anywhere, in any
position, and usually within five minutes.

Sebastian's hair gleamed black in the light. A strand fell
over his forehead, making him seem boyish and vulnerable. A
burst of confetti shot through my stomach as I studied his profile. His face was relaxed, removing the near-constant frown
he wore. The corner of his mouth twitched. God, how I loved
the dark red color that flushed his lips. It was so unique, so
captivating.

A laugh echoed in my head. *Oh, Ari, you've got it bad.*

It was so much more than that, though. There was a connection, made by similarities. Even here in the craziness that was New 2, he was different, born of two very different families.

I watched his chest rise and fall. *He even breathes attractively.* I snorted softly at that. Not a thought Ari Selkirk had ever had before, and one she'd die before admitting out loud.

Still smiling, I closed my eyes. Yeah, New 2 was affecting me in all kinds of bizarre ways.

I woke to darkness, my head on Sebastian's chest, his arms wrapped around me. A peek at the windows told me that dawn had yet to break over the city. My eyes closed again, ignoring the part of my mind that said, *Get up!*, too comfortable with the warmth of Sebastian's body and the smell of skin, like the scent of water from a crystal-clear lake in the Tennessee mountains.

His hand twitched on my arm, sending a chill racing down my skin. He was waking. *Damn.* He cleared his throat softly. I lifted my head and sat back as he scooted to a more upright position. I yawned and stretched my arms, avoiding his gray eyes and feeling a little self-conscious at having gravitated toward him in sleep.

The creaks overhead meant that Henri was up.

Sebastian peered closely at his watch, his eyes not yet adjusted to waking, his hair rumpled and cute. I smiled.

"Shit. We need to go," he muttered, shoving the gown's skirt from his legs, removing his feet from the table, and then leaning forward, elbows on his knees, black hair falling into his eyes.

Footsteps banged on the stairs, way too many to be from one person. Henri entered the room with Dub, Crank, and Violet on his heels. "I already told them they couldn't come with us."

Dub snorted. "I don't know what you've been smoking, Henri, or what *world* you're living in, but no one tells us what to do."

Violet and Crank both nodded in agreement. Pascal was tucked under Violet's arm, and she was back in her usual black dress, a Mardi Gras mask propped atop her head.

I stood, straightening my gown. "I need to change."

I left them to figure it out while I went upstairs and changed into the clothes that Michel had left out for me during my stay in the Quarter. Once that was done, I made sure the blade was in my backpack.

Sebastian was just zipping up his bag as I jogged down the stairs. The others stood by the front door with grim, determined faces. "I take it we're all going?" I said.

"It's a free country." Sebastian slung his bag over his shoulder. "If anyone gets hurt, Charity Hospital is nearby."

As the others headed outside and down Coliseum Street, I paused. 1331 First Street in the misty darkness before dawn was an awesome sight. A black, hulking shadow. An eerie, silent giant that guarded the ravaged streets. I gave it a respectful nod.

This was home. And I loved it.

I'd be forever grateful for what Bruce and Casey had done for me, but Memphis was not the place for me. More than anything I wanted to stay here, to make a life in the GD. On my terms. Not on the Novem's terms.

Whether I would ever have that opportunity was yet to be decided, though. There was the little matter of getting the Novem and the Greek goddess of war off my back.

"Ari!" Dub called.

With one parting look, I hurried down the street, catching up with the others and falling into step with Sebastian. "So, what did you mean before about anyone getting hurt?"

"Part of the cemetery was flooded during the storms. A portion of it sank some. It hasn't drained."

Henri laughed. "Lafayette *Swamp* Cemetery is more like it. City of the Dead. Land of the Creepy Crawlies."

A hard shiver raced straight up my spine to the back of my neck. I shuddered. Great.

"Like I said, if anyone gets bit, the hospital isn't far away."

But which part of the cemetery held the bones of Alice Cromley?

I didn't ask, not really wanting to know. Get in, get out. That's what I needed to focus on. With our group, maybe we'd scare away any "creepy crawlies" before they got too close.

A brush on my arm made me glance down to see Violet, Pascal's head bobbing up and down with her small steps. "I hope it's in the swampy part," she murmured with a wistful expression.

O-kay. Maybe you should keep Violet by your side. If there were any snakes, she and Pascal could take care of them. Actually, that wasn't a bad idea. Violet was going to stay right by my side.

Lafayette Cemetery No. 1 was four blocks over from First Street. The approaching dawn had turned the inky sky to a dull purple, enough light to see, but also enough to cast shadows in dark places and illuminate the long, silvery moss that hung from the oaks and cypress trees inside and outside of the cemetery. Through the tall wrought-iron fence, tombs were visible, rising like gray ghosts from the soft ground. The gate whined loudly as Henri pushed it open, the sound making my pulse rise.

The smell of wet stone and mud hung heavy in the dewy air, reminding me of the plantation house on the Mississippi. Leaves and debris littered the grounds around the main gate. Thick, bushy vines grew over the iron arch. I ducked under the vines and stepped onto what had once been a paved lane, but now it was cracked and covered with moss and weeds.

The only sound was the shuffle of our footsteps as we disturbed the hallowed ground. Long rows of tombs, carved to resemble miniature churches of marble and stone, ran down either side of the lane.

Time and the hurricanes had left their mark, leaving discoloration, fractures, and broken marble strewn all over. Some tombs had been lifted by the flood tides and carried to a high rubble pile against the fence. Within the rubble and vines and leaves were human bones and funerary pieces left to the elements.

I watched Sebastian's back, wondering what had been so important for him to have come to a place like this to search out Alice Cromley.

Henri stopped at the end of one long alley. Sebastian continued past him, turning down another cluttered row where tombs closed in around us. There was enough light now to reveal small details on the ground. I tripped, distracted by a broken skull stuck under a slab of marble.

Dub gave me a gentle push over a rubble pile. "Don't bother," he said, noting the direction of my gaze, but mistaking my reasons for looking. "The place has been picked clean."

"What do you mean?"

"You know. The stuff they were buried with. Rings. Necklaces. Keepsakes. I found a giant ruby in that one over there."

"You stole from a tomb?" I knew Dub was a grave robber. Sebastian had told me, but I couldn't seem to get past the idea.

He shrugged and kicked a small bit of marble from the path. "Sure. Not like they're gonna need it. Where do you think we got all that stuff last night? We sell it to Spits, he sells it to antique shops, and they sell it to the tourists."

The idea of unsuspecting tourists walking around wearing a dead person's jewelry gave me the willies. My thoughts went to the bedroom I'd slept in. "Please tell me that skull upstairs is not real."

Crank laughed over her shoulder, her pigtail braids sticking out from the back of her cabbie hat. "That's Eugene Hood from Saint Louis Number One."

St. Louis No. 1 was a cemetery in the French Quarter. No wonder the skull had unnerved me; it was real!

I ducked under a low branch that had fallen across the tombs. The alley dead-ended at the tall iron fence that surrounded the cemetery. Sebastian ducked around the corner of a tomb, following the fence line down the soft carpet of leaves and grass until the ground became soft and squishy, and the scent of swamp grew stronger.

Up ahead, rows and rows of tombs rose out of the black, brackish water.

Sebastian turned again, filling me with relief. At least we weren't going *forward*.

The squish, squish, squish of our steps became louder.

My relief was short-lived as the thought of sinking into mud riddled with corpses, set my stomach clenching and my nerves on edge.

"Here it is," Sebastian said quietly, stopping and facing a tomb. Two steps led to a six-foot-tall iron door, both sides framed with marble urns filled with sludge, debris, and a few tufts of grass. The tomb was covered in lichen and algae. The inscription on the door read: THE RIVER ANGELS, 1867.

Black water seeped over the toes of my boots the longer I stood in one spot. Violet let Pascal down, and the alligator scurried away, probably off to hunt for breakfast.

I glanced behind me to the dark, shadowy swamp, seeing the faint glow of eyes, dozens of eyes, and hoping to hell they were frogs or alligators.

Henri helped Sebastian shove the heavy iron door inward until the space was big enough to squeeze through. Then he stood back and wiped his hands. "I'm staying out here this time. Y'all have fun."

Sebastian let his bag slide off his shoulder, unzipped it, and pulled out a fat vanilla-colored candle. "Dub."

Dub snapped his fingers over the wick. Flame licked into the air as Sebastian faced me. "Ready?"

One last glance over my shoulder revealed that more glowing eyes had appeared, rows and rows of them, tiny dots bobbing in the water. Watching and waiting. I moved forward, suppressing a hard shudder and shaking off the bizarre idea that those glowing eyes had come for me.

Deep breaths. Long one in. Long one out.

I stepped up the cracked marble steps as Sebastian entered the tomb, leaving a small orange light for me to follow.

I angled my body, slipping easily inside.

The musty, damp air made it hard to breathe. About eight feet deep and maybe seven feet high at its vaulted peak, the tomb was big enough for four, maybe five people to stand with elbow room.

On each of the rectangular sides were two long shelves stacked with urns and funerary boxes. More had been stacked on the floor beneath the shelves.

"The tombs were reused over and over. That's why there are so many bodies here. Back in the old days, they'd remove the bones from the latest coffin, put them into one of those boxes, and then bring in a new coffin with a new dead body. Once the body inside was decayed or another family member died, they'd repeat the process. Kind of like musical chairs for the dead."

"Nice." I looked around the small space, noticing that the older funerary boxes were cracked and rotting, bones peeking through. My heart pounded, because I was trying like hell not to draw the smell of decaying corpses into my lungs. "Which one was Alice?"

Sebastian walked to the very back of the tomb, where what I thought was a long marble seat was actually a stone coffin lining the back wall. Above it, in a niche carved into the marble wall, was an old half-burnt candle covered in rot.

"You just said they moved the bones into the boxes."

"All but this one. That legend you heard from the carriage driver . . . the two bodies in the river? Just a story." He placed the candle on the small niche shelf and then knelt at the tomb. "Help me push." He took a spot at one corner while I knelt at the other, placing my hands on the rough marble lid.

"Okay, so what's the real story then?"

"Alice Cromley was killed by her lover. A crime of passion. No one knows for sure exactly what happened, except that she wasn't dumped in the river, and as she lay dying, she gave him instructions on how to prepare her body. Some voodoo ritual. He did as she asked, afraid of being cursed, and because, some say, he really did love her. Ready?"

I nodded, knowing I'd have to breathe soon. As it was, my lungs and heart could barely keep up. My teeth clenched as I faced the stone, finally dragging in a deep breath, knowing it was better to do it now than when the coffin was open and the air filled with . . . Alice Cromley.

The weight of the marble lid had us both sweating by the time we managed to angle the top part. Once that was done, we went to the other end and did the same, until the coffin was opened almost halfway.

Sebastian sat back. Sweat dampened his hairline. "That should do it." He swiped his forearm over his brow before standing up to retrieve the candle. He gazed down into the coffin, his profile grim.

I rose up on my knees, tall enough to see over the ledge of the coffin and down into the final resting place of the infamous Alice Cromley.

I gasped. Both hands flailed around for support, something, anything to keep me from falling backward. I gripped the end of the rough coffin.

A perfectly preserved, very beautiful Creole woman lay inside.

Alice Cromley.

Her dress was in decayed shreds, but her skin and hair looked like she'd been put in the stone coffin only hours earlier.

"This is impossible," I whispered.

A chuckle made me turn away from the macabre scene, to find Sebastian grinning at me with one black eyebrow raised. "After all you've seen? Vampires. A goddess. A *harpy*."

"Yeah, and every single one is impossible. Just like this."

Sebastian's chuckle sounded wrong in our current predicament. "Not in New 2. In New 2 anything is possible."

"Even defeating a Greek goddess?"

Sebastian unzipped his bag. "We should hurry before the sun rises." He pulled out garden shears.

"Jesus." My stomach went from tense to sickened in a flash.

"Guess that means I'll be doing the honors."

Apparently he hadn't expected anything else, because he was already turning toward the coffin. He leaned inside and lifted Alice Cromley's bare foot. I noticed she was missing a little toe.

Shit. Shit. Shit.

I turned away and flinched. The snap of bone between the shears bounced off the marble walls. Any minute it would wake the dead. The angry dead, angry for defiling one of their own. I almost fled the tomb.

"Quickly," Sebastian whispered, sitting down with his back against the sarcophagus and pulling out the mortar and pestle from the backpack, skinning the small toe bone and then drying the piece and dropping it into the bowl. He began grinding, glancing up to see me on my feet and standing very still. "You want to know or not?"

I swallowed, forcing down the panic and fear that made my limbs numb and weak. Everything in me was shouting, *Run.* Run far, far away from this dark, nightmarish scene and never look back, never remember. But instead I sat woodenly on the floor as Sebastian continued to grind the tiny piece of bone.

Somewhere in the back of my mind I knew the contents of that bowl were going to find a home inside my body. But I didn't think about it. Just watched and let my mind go blank.

Seventeen

AFTER SEVERAL LONG MINUTES, SEBASTIAN TAPPED THE PESTLE against the rim of the mortar bowl, sending a minuscule shower of bone powder back into the bowl. "Hold out your hand."

My nostrils flared. I didn't move. I couldn't. My gaze locked onto Sebastian's, his gray eyes deep and unreadable. A tick flexed his jaw. Just one, but I saw it. Then he reached out, grabbed my hand, and dumped the contents into my palm.

"It freaked me out too," he said quietly. "But I'd do it again, if I needed to. It's just bone. Dust. No taste at all. It's like inhaling a pulverized rock."

"Pulverized rock," I repeated. *Pulverized rock. I can handle that. I'm strong. Can handle anything. Yes, anything.*

I trained my mind on the small quarter-size amount of powder in my cupped palm. *Pulverized rock.* I brought it closer, heart pounding against my rib cage, leaned down, and then inhaled.

It swept through my nasal passages and hit the back of my throat, grainy and . . . like rock, as Sebastian said. It gagged me. Too dry against an already arid throat. I couldn't swallow. It clumped together. My stomach gave a sickening wave, wanting to vomit, sending the signal to my throat just as my vision swam and a tingling sensation surged through my body, snaking under my skin like lightning.

The tomb tilted, rolling over like a carnival fun house.

The side of my face hit the floor. No, not the floor. Sebastian's hand, which softened my landing and then gently slid out from under my cheek.

My eyes were fixed, my view on the long glow of the candle, which sat on the floor, Sebastian's knee in one corner and the shadowed bone boxes in the darkness beyond.

I was frozen, completely paralyzed, but my mind kept rolling, kept circling slowly on the fun ride. My eyelids grew heavier and lower, finally able to close in a burst of white.

Bright flashes.

Bits of color. Glaring colors. Shimmering whites and vibrant blues.

The sun's reflection blinking and beaming off the sea, beaming off smooth marble.

Broken voices.

Snapshots of a Greek temple, jutting up from the rocks by the sea. Beautiful, this place. So beautiful.

Inside those perfect columns, white hair flies out, waving like a flag in the breeze.

My chest tightens. Fear flows through my system, propelled by the realization of what is happening. That it feels as though it's happening to me. The horror as the woman with the white hair jerks away from the large hand holding her arm. She loses her balance and trips as she flees inside the temple. She's too scared to feel the pain of her fall on the hard, unforgiving mosaic tiles. She turns, scooting back on her bottom, desperate, as the large figure looms above her.

She knows.

He wants her, and there is no way to stop this.

His hand reaches down and slowly pulls the hem of her dress up over her thighs. There is nothing she can do, nothing at all as the figure above her speaks soothing, foreign words adorned with power, the kind of power that tells her to keep her eyes down and not look into his face. That would surely mean death.

My fists clench, my entire body goes rigid and numb.

A slow, furious scream builds in the deepest part of me, born of rage, injustice, and fear. It tears from my throat, ringing with desperation and denial.

From some small, dark place in my mind where I can still reason, I know what is happening to the woman. But I refuse to experience those emotions, so I brace myself against it, against the power of Alice Cromley's clairvoyant bones, and fight hard, closing my mind to the emotions even as I see the flashes of the woman's rape in my mind.

And then it's over.

The woman on the floor curls up and weeps, her silvery hair spilling out in an arc on the colorful mosaic floor, her white gown blood-stained along the curve of her bottom, her body trembling.

My anger becomes hotter, taking on the anguish of the scene in my mind. My throat closes, and my eyes and cheeks are wet.

Another bright flash consumes the image.

A voice. A voice so familiar that it sends chills up my spine.

Athena.

I know the voice, though not the words. Those are like his. Foreign, but not hidden in false comfort. The images bounce quickly. And the words are brutal, condemning, and righteous. Disbelief slides into me like honey as I feel the woman's shock and a deep sense of foreboding. The goddess is blaming her for the rape in the temple, for defiling Athena's sacred place.

The woman pushes herself to her feet, sore, confused, heart-broken to be forsaken by the goddess she has worshipped and loved since childhood.

I see through the woman's eyes. Athena's feet and the bottom of her robe. Never her face. Not permitted to look upon the face of the gods. And then the curse begins. The words issuing from Athena's mouth are no more understood than before, but there is no mistaking this moment. This is the moment that the air charges and snaps with primeval energy, where it curls around the woman, rustling her gown and lifting her hair. This is where her eyes, her beauty, her hair are her downfall, where a vengeful and unjust goddess takes out her petty jealousies on an innocent, peaceful woman.

First raped and now blamed.

The woman screams as the very air itself enters her body, an air alive with Athena's words of power. It invades her skin, her organs, and her bones. It reshapes and brings forth ugliness and poison. The searing pain rips from her throat in a guttural, primal scream that makes me stop breathing. I feel this pain. But I know it is nothing like the real thing. She bends at the waist, and her stomach empties its contents onto the mosaic tiles. Pain has taken her vision. She no longer sees, only feels. Her scalp burns, breaking open in jerks and tears. She reaches up to grab her blistering head, but her hands are bitten by something. Painful bites. Over and over and over again until she is consumed by merciful blackness.

Breathe, I tell myself. My heartbeat pounds like a frenzied ritual drum, echoing inside me. Trapped.

Another flash takes me from the white temple to a dark cave. A shadowed place. A place where candlelight flickers on the walls, and the *screams and pants of the same woman echo through the hollow place.*

So much agony.

And then the cries of a newborn child as it is carried through the darkness by its mother, a new mother racked with the pain of childbirth. Heart pumping. Limbs so weak, but her will so strong. To save this child. To get this child away. Away. She weeps hot tears and her heart breaks with each step, with each step closer to abandoning her child.

But it's the only way.

She's been hiding for many months, and soon they will find her. And when they do, they will have no mercy on this child. This child born of woman and god.

I moan, my own voice reaching beyond the images to my ears as the child is laid at the doorstep of a small stone farmhouse.

And then the woman flees. Heart racing. Body weak and bleeding from childbirth, the warm liquid running down her thighs as fast as the tears roll down her face. She's done. This act of saving her child has broken her more than anything that Athena or the god ever did.

She returns to the cave, to the small nook where her child, a daughter, first breathed life, and she digs her hands into the earth to cover the afterbirth, to hide any evidence that a child has been born. And then she lies down like the monster she is to wait for the hunter.

This time she won't hide, won't run or fight. This time she will let him take her head as the others have tried to do. She is tired, too damaged to go on.

She doesn't know how many nights and days she lay there on the cold, rocky ground of the cave, but she knows immediately when another invades her space. She lifts her head and shivers as the monster in her wakes. Her hands feel for the small candle and flint, and she lights the wick.

Shadows lick and writhe on the walls, revealing a man in battle gear creeping closer. His hand flexes around the hilt of a short sword. His other hand lifts a round shield as he approaches the candlelight.

The shadows on the wall meet.

She bows to the sound of hissing in her ears, a sound she hates more than anything. A sound that will soon be silenced.

He swings.

The sharp sting on the back of her neck pulls a gasp from her lips, but then relief flows through her. She is finally free. Free of the curse, free of being a monster. She welcomes her death with the comforting memories of her child nestled in her arms.

"Ari!" The back of my head rolled from side to side on the hard floor. Hands gripped both shoulders hard. "Ari! Goddamn it, breathe!"

Sebastian's voice. Sebastian's hands. *Breathe.* Why? I was

fine. Everything was fine. Sleepy and fine. I settled back into the numbing, warm blackness that I found so comforting.

Until a fist slammed into my chest.

Fuck!

My eyes flew open. I sat up, mouth open, eyes wide but unseeing. My lungs burned. The pain over my heart, brutal. My mouth gaped like a fish out of water. Suffocating. My vision sharpened and with it came the realization that I needed to inhale, to breathe.

Jesus Christ, I needed to breathe!

My body lurched as my brain finally fired the correct signal, and I was able to suck in a long, desperate draught of air. My heart pistoned so hard, one breath was not enough, not nearly enough.

Sebastian sat back and wiped a hand over his forehead, his eyes filling with relief as he grabbed my hand.

After a long while, he said, "You stopped breathing. You were so still and quiet. The whole time. You didn't even blink."

A series of shudders went through me. I bit back tears and swallowed. "I didn't?" I gasped. Because I sure as hell remembered screaming and crying and moaning.

And I sure as hell remembered my past. No, not *my* past. My ancestor's cruel, heartbreaking past. My chest ballooned with the lingering despair I'd experienced as my ancestor. My head fell into my hands.

"You saw."

I glanced up at Sebastian, hands falling limp into my lap. "Yeah," I answered, voice ragged and small. "I saw." He waited. And I couldn't make the words come. "Do you mind if we get out of here?"

He eyed me for a long moment, and I saw worry and fear in his look, but that was all, just a brief glimpse before his head dipped and he began packing the contents of our ritual into his bag.

After shoving the heavy lid over the unnatural corpse of Alice Cromley, we left the tomb.

Long streaks of purple and orange leaked across the dark sky from the east, revealing the cemetery in all its creepy, broken glory. The high iron fence rose like battlefield spikes, keeping in the undefeated tombs, the ruins, and the mossy, exposed bones.

Still weak and numb, I made my way carefully down the two broken steps, my eyes coming to rest on the backs of the others. Odd. I thought they'd be facing me, waiting, curious to know what had happened.

Four in a line. Shoulder to shoulder. No one moved.

"Guys?" I said slowly, the hairs on my arms rising.

"Shh!" Henri's head moved slightly, the only indication that the sound had come from him.

I exchanged a quick, confused glance with Sebastian before

stepping closer to see what had grabbed their attention.

A gasp lodged in my throat.

No.

Snakes. At least thirty of them. All on the edge of the swamp, where water met ground. Bobbing in the water. Gathered. Drawn there. Eyes on the tomb. On me. *Looking at me.*

I stumbled back, falling against the steps. Pain lanced though my back and elbow as they cracked against marble. One look was all it took, one brief look that would be burned into my brain forever. And fear, the likes of which I'd never known before, swept me up and propelled me back. Scrambling, falling hard to my knees, my hands scraping across the jagged edges of a broken stone as I continued, turning and running.

Run.

My heart and lungs grew strained with the force of terror pushing the blood through my system, making me tingly and unsteady even as I darted around tombs and leaped over ruins, slowing only when the gate that led to freedom rose up before me.

I paused in front of the overgrown gate, my chest heaving, my arms going limp at my sides, the backpack slipping out of my hand and falling to the ground. Tears flowed down my cheeks and neck as I struggled to breathe and process what I'd just witnessed.

A nightmare. A horrible fucking nightmare.

The quick footsteps of the others approaching made me swipe hastily at the tears.

Crank was the first to reach me. "You okay?"

"Yeah. I'm fine."

"You're afraid of snakes." Dub arrived next, sitting on a stone.

Sebastian tossed his backpack at Dub's feet and joined him on the stone, drawing one leg up, his voice even and quiet. "Never seen them do that before."

A small, ironic laugh stopped short of my mouth, turning into a harsh sound in my throat. Yeah. Neither had I. I placed my hands on my hips, wanting to toss my head back and scream, but instead I stayed silent, staring at the sky as it transitioned from dawn to day.

My body convulsed with a violent quake. I rubbed my face hard, trying to rub out the vision in my mind, and the horrifying realization that the snakes had come to see *me*. To pay homage to their queen. Medusa. Gorgon. The one who carried the curse of my family and would one day become a monster. A hideous creature so reviled one look would turn a person to stone. Stone as hard as the one Dub and Sebastian sat on.

That was my legacy. *That* was what awaited me.

And it was fucked up enough to scare even a goddess. It figured. I laughed.

"So?" Henri said, winded, having finally made it to the gate. "What'd you see in the tomb?"

"Nothing." My voice was laced with horror and grief.

Violet came strolling up, Pascal under her arm once again. I couldn't look at those reptilian eyes, so I turned back, coming face-to-face with Henri's frown and Crank's incredulous look.

"We just came all the way out here with you and you're not going to tell us?"

"I didn't ask you to come, Crank." I winced, knowing I sounded like a first-rate asshole. "I'm sorry, it's just . . . I can't . . ." How could I tell them? How could I tell them and watch their faces turn into shock and disgust?

"You never would've figured this out without our help," Henri pointed out. "We deserve to know what you're up against. If Athena goes on the warpath, it affects us all."

"It doesn't if I'm not here."

Crank's eyes widened in disbelief, and her hands curled into two small fists. "So, what are you saying? You're going to leave us?"

I tossed my hands up, staring hard at a point beyond Crank's shoulder. I didn't know what the hell I was saying anymore. Just that I couldn't tell them what I was, what I would become. I couldn't watch them run away, turn their backs on me—the biggest misfit of them all, forsaken even by those in New 2. And if *that* happened, then where was I supposed to go? Where the hell would anyone accept me?

No, this secret would go with me to the grave if it had to. Whether it meant hurting my friends or not, no matter if it meant leaving New 2 and never looking back.

A squawk interrupted my thoughts, reverberating through the thin morning air.

A raven landed on the peak of a nearby tomb, its wings fluttering for a moment before folding behind its back.

"Ari," Sebastian said, "whatever it is, you can tell us."

The raven cawed again, the sound echoing Sebastian's last two words. *Tell us! Tell us!* Almost as though it laughed at me. God, I was losing it.

But then, the others were staring strangely at the bird too.

I wasn't the only one who heard.

Tell us! Tell us!

Dread swept beneath my skin as the raven transformed into a black-clad woman perched on her haunches on the peak of the tomb, her hands curling over the edge, fingernails long and vicious, a wicked grin on her lips. "Yes, tell us, Ari. Tell what you have seen."

Athena.

Dead flowers and flashing emerald beads threaded through her tangled, upswept hair.

A hard swallow went down my throat, followed by a tightening of every muscle I possessed. All the emotions of my vision boiled over, as fresh and furious as they'd been a few moments ago. "You should know, you petty piece of shit."

I blinked, surprised by the venom and the words that came out of my mouth. But I knew where they came from. From seeing Medusa, and the horror she had gone through. And for what? For being beautiful? For being raped by some ass-wipe of a god in Athena's perfect temple?

Fuck Athena.

Athena's eyes narrowed to fine points. She cocked her head. But the rise in her chest as she breathed told me that the words had cut. Good.

"Well, then," the goddess said, her perfect lips twitching, "if you won't tell them, perhaps I should."

Eighteen

"No!" I shouted as Athena eased her legs down so that she straddled the roofline of the tomb, her feet dangling over the edge and swinging like a child's. Her smug smile chilled me to the bone. "Please," I whispered, hating myself for begging. "Don't."

"Ooh!" She clapped her hands together. "I know. How about we just show them instead? A little taste of what's to come. Just a vision, not enough to hurt them. And just enough to show *you*, dear Ari, that you don't belong here."

Oh God.

I sank to my knees. "No," my voice choked. "Please. Don't do this."

One corner of her mouth twisted up smugly. I knew it was

too late. I saw it in the brutal glint and the incredible arrogance lighting the depths of her eyes.

Athena's hands shot out, and from them came two shafts of crackling, green-tinged bolts. I didn't even have time to stand, just stayed frozen on my knees as her power swirled around me, ruffling my clothing and lifting the wisps of my hair. The knot at the back of my head broke free. My hair lifted and spread out in white waves. My stomach clenched as I tried to double over, to curl into myself and hide, but an invisible force held me still, held my chin high and my shoulders straight. I fought against it, sweat breaking out on the small of my back.

I screamed, trying to lift my hands, to hold my hair down, to stop what was happening, but they wouldn't cooperate. My knees lifted off the ground and I spun, facing the pale, stunned faces of my friends. Arms wide, completely open. No way to hide.

And Sebastian—Sebastian, who had one foot in front of him, was pressing forward but unable to move, unable to help. None of them able to move.

The only action I could make was with my eyes. They connected with Sebastian's and grew glassy. My throat closed. My heart pumped at a frantic, painful pace. Then my hair began to separate into several twisted and swaying strands. My scalp burned fire.

Dear God, I'm on fire!

I shrieked—a horrible sound. I squeezed my eyes closed, forcing it to stop. *Please! Just stop!*

And then I felt them stirring beneath my scalp. My mouth fell open as I gasped for air that would not come. Revulsion shuddered through me, making my nerves electric with fear. Tears leaked hot from my eyes. *No! No! No!*

My scalp split, and it felt like smooth, round smoke slid up and out of my skin, turning and twisting around strands of my hair and becoming vague shadows of living things. Terrifying, living things. Smoky visions of what was to come. Writhing, twining together, a halo of sickening, milky white, yellow, and orange apparitions.

My eyes rolled back into my head. My heart thudded hard, one last time, unable to support the panic-driven adrenaline coursing through my veins. My eyes popped open against my will, Athena forcing me to watch. To see my friends.

My friends.

Backing up. Reaching out to one another for support. Horror whitening their stricken faces and dragging their mouths open.

No, I wanted to beg. *Please don't go.*

But I couldn't speak.

And Sebastian. Sebastian who had that one foot out, trying to break the invisible barrier and help me, stepped back.

He stepped back.

My chest deflated, sinking in, collapsing as the truth and the cold realization gripped the last remnants of hope I had and smashed them into smithereens. It shouldn't have surprised me, really. Don't get your hopes up and you don't get hurt. Don't trust or love and you don't get hurt. I'd broken my own rules. And what sane or even slightly sane person wouldn't run, or shit themselves, or become shell-shocked? I couldn't blame them.

Crank held on to Henri's arm, her face pressed against it, eyes as round as Frisbees. They all backed away. All but Violet, who stood amazed, slowly pushing up her Mardi Gras mask to reveal an expression of childlike wonder.

Henri rushed forward and grabbed Violet, jerking her back. She whipped around and bared her tiny fangs at him. He dropped her as though burned.

They were through the gate now, fingers wrapping around the bars and yelling at Violet to come, the voices muted and drowning in the chaos that swirled through my brain, mixing with the pain and the heartbreak.

In an act of defiance, Violet sat cross-legged on the ground. They finally gave up. Henri pulled Crank and Dub away from the bars and ran down the street. Sebastian hesitated, giving one last unfathomable look at me, hovering inside the cemetery, and then he hurried after the others.

Athena released me. A breath whooshed from my lungs as

the weight of my body hit the ground, sinking into the softness. The side of my face slapped against the wet earth, and it felt good, that chill.

I stayed unmoving, too weak and too hurt to care.

Athena's feet hit the ground and sauntered the few short steps to where I lay. Her booted toe shoved my shoulder, pushing me onto my back.

I gazed up at the face of the goddess, the cruel bitch who had a special place in hell, if such a place existed. She dropped down on her haunches and tenderly wiped the single stream of tears from the left side of my face, then rested her elbows on her knees. "You don't belong here, child. *They* don't want you. *He* doesn't want you. Even the misfits have rejected you. There is no place for you in New 2, no place anywhere in this world that will accept you for what you are. Your home is with me."

My chest tightened with the most intense despair and loneliness. Athena was right. The Bitch was right.

"You have until dusk to decide. Come home with me, daughter of Medusa. I will give you shelter, riches, your heart's desire. You have but to submit to my rule, that is all." She reached out and lifted a strand of my hair, rubbing it through her fingers, a flash of envy and bitterness passing through her eyes. "What will you do when you turn? Where will you go? Perhaps . . . perhaps after a time I shall lift this curse from your body and give you your life back. Be a good girl, Aristanae, a good little minion, and I just might."

Another trail of tears followed in the same wet path as Athena stood and disappeared.

I let my eyes close, rolled my body so that it was curled onto one side, pulled my legs and arms in, and cried silently into the wet grass.

Everything hurt. The outside. The inside. And I finally understood what it felt like to be broken. I let the anguish consume me and take me into a world of numb desolation.

After a long moment, Violet sat down behind me and snuggled against my back. The small act hurt so badly, fresh tears flowed. Violet. Little Violet had accepted me, had shown mercy and kindness and loyalty.

I woke to heat at my back and the lukewarm drizzle of rain on my face. Slowly, every muscle protesting, I pushed myself up onto my hip and gazed over my shoulder to see Violet curled up on the grass, with Pascal stretched out beside her. The kid's hand rested lightly on the leaves beside her face, the exposed wrist and hand so thin and fragile.

I rubbed the dryness from my puffy eyes and waited for my vision to return. Memories flooded me instead. Of my past, my curse, and what Athena had done to me to bend my will.

A depressed sigh escaped me as I gathered my long hair and shoved it over my shoulder. Now I understood why my mother had ended her life, why so many before her had done the same. I knew why the harpy had fled into the swamp, rather than back to civilization. Being alone was far better than seeing the frightened, horrified faces of those around you, those you cared for.

Music drifted through the cemetery, faint and crass. A brass band. Trumpet. Drums. Cymbals.

Violet's nose twitched. Her black lashes moved against pale skin. Her small hand dipped into the softness of the ground and she pushed herself up. She tucked her black bob behind one ear and then tilted her small face toward the misty sky.

I scooted back some. Dampness had seeped through my clothes and onto my skin. The drizzle gathered and ran down the side of my face. "Violet, why did you stay?"

Pascal waddled into Violet's lap. Her slim fingers stroked his back as she turned her face away from the drizzle, large black eyes full of weight and mystery. "I thought you looked beautiful."

Fresh pain squeezed my sore heart. I swallowed down the tears that wanted to rise again and instead gave a small laugh. "Thanks." Only Violet, only this small Gothic doll with a penchant for reptiles and sequins was willing to accept me.

The time I had spent with Violet since coming to New 2 was short, but from those first interactions, there was a connection.

One, I think, that stemmed from our uniqueness, from recognizing a kindred soul. Her staying here with me. Her acceptance of me. I knew then that I'd do anything for her.

"The parade is coming," she said. "The kids' parade. We were supposed to be in it." Her head angled toward the music. "It's almost dusk."

Goose bumps sprouted along my cold thighs and arms. The drizzle had forced a low mist to the ground, a thin gray shroud upon the grass. The sky above was lost in a sea of haze and thick clouds. The gnarled branches of the oak tree nearby spread out like dark lightning across the sky.

"She'll be back soon," Violet said. "What are you going to do?"

I glanced at the tomb where Athena had appeared. "I don't know."

"You should kill her."

"Me. Kill a goddess." *Right.*

Violet shrugged and got to her feet, wiping the grass and bits of stone and debris from her black dress and her hair before righting the mask on her head, leaving it up so her face was still visible.

The music became louder, but the mist hid the Mardi Gras revelers. I stood, shaking out my long hair and shivering despite myself. Knowing what I was, what I'd become . . . I wondered how many of my ancestors had actually been able to live with the change, with being a monster, rather than end their own lives. And how many had died by the sword of the τέρας hunters? In the end, the outcome was always the same. So why had Athena decided to spare me?

Going with Athena seemed like my only option. That or disappearing. *And where will you go? How can you live with those things on you?* Those things that inspired more fear in me than death itself.

Violet bumped me. "She's here."

I whirled. Athena perched on the long, thick branch of the oak tree. She jumped down and strolled over. "Have you come to a decision, gorgon?"

This thing, this *goddess* had caused so much death and heartache to my family, to thousands of women over the centuries. I knew, in that moment, I could never give in. I'd rather die like all the others. But more than that, I'd rather have vengeance. "Go fuck yourself, Athena."

Violet grabbed my hand, squeezing tightly. I wanted to shove her back, to tell her to run, but doing that would draw Athena's attention to the child.

Athena struck me across the cheek so quickly, I didn't even have time to tense. The hot sting and shock sent a gasp through my mouth. My ears rang, and pain shot through my face.

Slowly I righted myself, grinding my teeth together and

clenching my fists as I faced the tall goddess. Athena grabbed my chin, squeezing hard, and leaned down close to my face. Her eyes gleamed with an impossible inner light, a beautiful sight if one could get past the cruel twist of her lips. "You should watch your mouth, little one. Or I shall put your head on a stake like I did your mother's."

"My mother killed herself," I ground out, furious that she'd even mentioned my mother.

"And I claimed her body. She looked quite nice outside my temple."

Anger flashed bright and white behind my eyelids. I swung with all my strength, but she caught my hand and leaned close even as I struggled. "You hear that sound, Aristanae? Those are your friends, those are the children of New 2 who are about to pass by this cemetery and die at the hands of my army."

Behind Athena's shoulder, I saw movement in the gray mist, movement that made the fog swirl, revealing bits and pieces, images of Athena's creations as they gathered from the fog. Lurking atop tombs, walking slowly over the ground, leaping from the tree limbs. Hideous, gnarled things. Things that looked as though Frankenstein himself had been at work. Athena's army.

"Those"—Athena tossed a nod over her shoulder, dropping her hand from my chin—"are your family now. Made, like your ancestor, of curses and power. They would worship you as a queen, you know. You belong with them. With me. Come, and I shall never set foot in New 2 again."

The parade music became louder. Closer. I flicked a glance over my shoulder, getting my first gray glimpse of the parade as it progressed slowly down the street beyond the iron fence. Soon they would pass the cemetery gate, and if Athena wasn't bluffing, they were all in danger.

I turned back to the goddess. "Why not just kill me like all the others?"

"Because you are different from the others, and I've found a better use for you." Her face softened somewhat. "You have the heart of a rebel, Ari. I was once the same, once wanted to fight battles I knew I couldn't win simply because the reason was just and right. But all those things, hope, innocence, optimism, faith . . . They are fleeting, and what do you have left? You must grow up, realize your place, and what is best. Swear fealty to me, and you will be safe."

My eyes narrowed as a strange sense of confidence rose in me. Athena was trying too hard to make her case and convince me. She'd given me all this time to decide, all this time alive, unharmed. A sharp burst of laughter bubbled into my throat. "You're really afraid of me, aren't you?"

Athena blinked and straightened. Her jaw twitched. "I am the Goddess of War, little child. I am afraid of no one, for I cannot die. I am Death, for I murdered the Goddess of Death in her bed. Best you remember that, for your friends are here."

The parade didn't pass by the gate, but turned beneath it instead. *What the hell?*

All masked. All on foot.

Shit.

The masked figures spread out behind me and Violet. The music stopped. My heart pounded as indecision gripped me. Had they gone crazy?

A black-clad figure in a cape strode forward and pushed up his mask. Sebastian. Our eyes locked. He nodded as a light breeze swept past me. Another figure stepped up. Michel. And then eight more. The Novem had come. And Dub, Henri, and Crank. All grim-faced. All prepared to fight.

They'd come back.

Reinforcements continued filing into the cemetery.

A soft blush appeared on Athena's cheeks as the goddess's angry eyes fixed on the revelers. "This is none of your business, Novem," she spat. "I made her. She's mine."

"She stopped being yours the moment you turned on your creation and had Medusa murdered. The gorgons have never been yours. They were their own, free to choose. Free to live," Michel said in a deep, confident voice, walking with Sebastian and the others to stand beside me.

The hideous line of monsters and humanoid creatures behind Athena hissed and fidgeted, ready to fight, to attack, to kill. My skin crawled.

"You would start a war over her?" Athena raged. "She is of no use to you. She is not mature. She has no power."

"No," said Josephine. "Not yet, but all we must do is protect her from you, and once her power comes, you will never be a threat to New 2 again."

Athena hissed loudly, her face shifting into death and then back again. "Then war it shall be."

"Heed your actions carefully, goddess," Michel said. "For we are evenly matched."

Athena ignored Michel and threw out her hands, tossing her head back and issuing a piercing supernatural war cry.

My eardrums vibrated as Sebastian grabbed my hand and jerked me and Violet away from the front line. The Novem and their family members rushed forward to engage Athena and her minions. Their speed was unnaturally fast. Their capes and limbs swirled the mist. Hideous things flew and fought and screeched. Red arced through the mist as blood flowed.

I pulled against Sebastian, tripping over marble as he ran. "Let me go!"

We reached the back of the line near the gate. "You can't stay here."

"I have to! This is my fight, Sebastian. I can't leave."

"You have to leave! They're giving their lives to protect you!"

I hesitated. Confusion settled on my shoulders. "Why?"

He moved closer. "My father told me everything. You're a god-killer, Ari."

"What?"

"Athena. When she cursed Medusa and gave her the power to turn anyone to stone, she forgot to exempt the gods. When she realized her mistake, she created the τέρας hunters to destroy Medusa and all the descendants after her. You alone have the power to turn her and any other god to stone."

"Then why didn't she just kill me like all the others?"

"Because before she held the power of the Aegis. It was a weapon that made it nearly impossible to defeat her. But she lost it, so now she needs you. A new weapon to destroy the other gods, to kill us, who the hell knows"—he shoved me—"but you have to run!"

Two creatures broke through the line. Sebastian ducked as one leaped at him. It sailed over his back and rolled. The other one swung a wicked-looking blade toward me. I ducked, kicked its knee, and then backhanded its face, spinning and lifting the sword from its hand, my momentum allowing me to complete a three-sixty and use the extra force to swing the blade down, beheading the creature.

Its head rolled into the mist.

Jesus! My heart hammered in disbelief at what I'd just done. But I didn't have time to think more. Another one came and I fought, yelling to Sebastian to get Violet and the other kids to safety. But Violet was already scurrying up one of the trees and the others were fighting, using their size to defeat or distract their opponents as the Novem and their families were using their own magic and abilities to fight.

Physical and brutal, the vampires attacked in a frenzy. I froze for a moment, seeing Gabriel—even without the mask, I knew it was him—tear a creature's throat out with his fangs, just as vicious as the shape-shifters' claws and jaws as they rushed the line. A figure rushed past, winked at me, leaped into the air, and shifted into a brown wolf before his paws ever landed on the ground. Hunter Deschanel. One of the guys I'd freed from Athena's prison.

And then my eyes found the goddess standing with a blade in each hand, working them with preternatural speed and cutting down any opponent who came her way. Her eyes glowed a deep, deep green.

Pain exploded in my skull.

I fell, not even seeing the blow from behind as a creature jumped on me. I shouted Sebastian's name, but he was engaged in a battle against two creatures. Rough hands flipped me over and found my throat, squeezing hard. I kicked, tried to roll, but to no avail. A gray, leathery face sneered at me. Hairless. Small holes for a nose. No lips, nothing to shield the rows of sharp tiny teeth that snapped at me.

And then I remembered Arachne and the harpy.

I needed to get his hands off my neck.

Gathering what little strength I had left, I kicked up with both legs, twisting my torso and catching the creature's head between my calves. I dragged him off with a downward thrust of my legs. As soon as the hands left my throat I screamed their names into the mist, adding every ounce of force I had to increase the volume.

"Mapsaura! Arachne!"

I felt the air change with the power of their names, charging, electrifying, and shooting into the clouds.

The creature ducked out from my pin. I turned to run, to yell their names again, but he grabbed my head with both hands, his claws digging into my temples. He had a firm grasp, pulling my head up, trying to disconnect the skull from the base of the spine. *Christ!* I couldn't hold on much longer, he was too strong. His arm slid around my neck, choking again.

My heart slowed. Pressure built in my face. All around me, the battle seemed to slow as my lungs failed.

Wind blew down, billowing the mist, scattering leaves and debris.

A loud, piercing screech rent the air.

I heard the flap of massive wings just before the creature on me was picked up. I was lifted two feet off the ground before he let go, and I fell onto my back and watched in shock as the mist tornadoed up, pulled by the wake of the harpy and her prey.

Three seconds later the creature's body came hurtling back to earth to break upon a tomb.

Mapsaura landed at my feet.

I gulped, gasping for air and completely stunned that my call had worked. "Thank you."

The small nostrils on the beak flared. The harpy's head swung around and froze, eyes zeroing in on Athena. And then I saw Arachne, flinging bodies left and right, trying to make it to the goddess who had imprisoned her for so long.

Mapsaura bent at the muscular knees and pushed off the ground, shooting straight up, disappearing into the mist, and then torpedoing down, aiming straight for Athena as Arachne broke free and made for the goddess.

Both creatures hit her at once.

But Athena wasn't the goddess of war for nothing. She caught each creature on a blade and used their momentum to throw them behind her. The harpy rolled herself right, finally stopping with her great talons digging a rut into the dirt. Mapsaura stretched her wings wide and a bone-chilling scream ripped from her throat, the sound almost as loud as Athena's war cry.

As Athena turned, distracted, a bolt of power from Michel and Sebastian, their hands combined, hit her square in the chest.

I blinked, storing away for another time the fact that Sebastian had *that* kind of power.

Athena flew back from the warlock blast as the harpy took flight again. Arachne lay on the ground, unmoving. But I saw Athena's quick realization. Her creatures were falling to the Novem. And here in New 2, her powers were diminished. She could be defeated.

"Fall back!" the goddess shouted, glancing up just in time to see the harpy barreling from the sky, her wings folded flat against her back.

Athena vanished.

Mapsaura's eyes went wide. Her wings unfurled and caught the air for two seconds before she rolled to the side, skimming the ground. Her talons punched into the soft soil, giving her enough room to flap her wings and push her high enough to skid-land atop one of the tombs. Slate roof tiles scattered as her talons dug in for support.

One by one Athena's creatures disappeared into the mist.

A hushed quality descended on the cemetery, the steady fall of rain becoming the dominant sound.

Bodies littered the ground. Moans and voices broke the eerie quiet. I made my way to Sebastian and Michel near the tomb where Mapsaura perched, but a broken body lay in my path. I stumbled. *Jesus.* It was Daniel. I dropped down next to him. Blood bubbled from a throat that had been ripped away. His eyes blinked rapidly. His mouth worked, trying to speak, but no sound came out.

"Oh my God, Daniel," I whispered, kneeling to help him but not knowing what to do. Josephine appeared next to me. "He'll live, right? He's a vampire. He'll live."

Two vampires, I think, walked forward and picked Daniel up. His head separated from his body, and the thin piece of skin holding him together ripped. My stomach rolled. I scooted back on my ass.

"He's already dead," Josephine said without a speck of emotion, and then walked away as the two men dumped Daniel's body, leaving him in a broken pile. A pile that suddenly collapsed into itself and turned to ash.

I gagged. Bile stung my throat. I swallowed it down, turning and staggering away from the ash as my gaze caught briefly on Violet scrambling down from the tree.

I focused on putting one foot in front of the other. Sebastian turned, seeing me approach. My eyes connected with his, and I opened my mouth just as a tingle of warning pricked my skin.

The hairs on my arms stood up.

Athena appeared at my back, instantly wrapping her arms around me. Her lips brushed the rim of my ear. "You know what they say." Her voice dropped to a deadly whisper. "If I can't have you . . . no one will." Her lips moved away from my ear. "Oh, and before you die, I want to thank you for leaving your father behind when you set the others free from my prison."

My insides shriveled. "What?"

She laughed. "Ironic, isn't it? A τέρας hunter falling in love with your mother, a gorgon, the very monster he was charged with killing. As your spirit leaves you, I want you to think of him, of all the things I have done to him for betraying me and not killing Eleni when he had the chance. All the things I am going to do to him now. Good-bye, little monster."

Athena shoved me away from her.

It seemed like it happened in slow motion. I stumbled to my knees, getting just a glimpse of the horror sliding over Sebastian's features and the blur that was Violet dropping out of the tree. Shock. I was in shock.

Athena raised a τέρας blade to take my head.

Time had slowed to the point that all the images of my life flashed randomly. But one image seemed to slow more than all the others—the image of me holding Athena's wrist at the Arnaud ball and making it turn to stone.

I had three and a half years left before maturing into a gorgon, but there was power inside me. I'd used it before, and that was the difference. I *was* different from all those before me. Time, evolution, the genes of my father . . . whatever the factors, I knew. I was a god-killer.

The blade sliced through the air. Somewhere in the back of my mind I heard a shout and a child's scream. But it didn't matter. It was happening too fast, too fast for any of them to help me. My blood hummed. My eyes locked onto the blade as it arced toward my neck.

I bowed my head and lifted my tingling hand, opening my palm, releasing all my anger, all the pain of my own life, my mother's life, and all of the pain I had felt as Medusa, my ancestor.

The blade met my hand.

And broke against stone.

The sound rang out in a deep, echoing pop, an exploding circle of power, the force of it flattening everyone to the ground. I raised my head as the broken part of the blade flew through the air, and I met Athena's astonished eyes.

My heart sounded slow and loud in my ears.

I shouldn't have been able to do that; I could see the same thought in Athena's stunned expression. Yet I had. My hand, I saw, was white like marble, white that was beginning to return to its fleshy color. I could control this power, and I didn't have to turn into some monster to use it.

Then Athena blinked. Time returned to normal at the same instant that Violet hit Athena's back from behind, her arms coming around the goddess's neck and her little fangs sinking into the skin as one of her hands lifted a small dagger and plunged it into Athena's heart.

A scream bubbled in Athena's throat.

Shock and dread sent me falling back on my ass as the shout of Violet's name, by many voices, echoed over the wet grounds.

And then they were gone.

Vanished, leaving behind the swirling mist. The hilt of Athena's broken blade dropped against a slab of marble as Violet's bloodied dagger thudded against the soft ground.

"Violet!" I screamed.

Nineteen

THREE DAYS HAD PASSED. THREE DAYS OF NO SLEEP AND NIGHT-mares and worry. Violet was gone. No one knew how to get her back. And no one had seen or heard from Athena.

Three days of going to the cemetery, calling for Pascal, searching every tomb, every crevice to find him. Violet would want that, and I owed her. I'd go every day until I found him.

Sebastian had spent the last two days in his room, banging on his drums, filling the house with such intense fury that it was difficult to stay there when he played.

Michel had sent a small force to the River Road planta-tion to rescue my father, but as expected, the prison was gone, like it had never existed. It'd been hard for Michel to do even that much. My father had killed innocent τέρας and humans of power in the name of Athena. But his love for my mother had changed him, had given him the power to go against the goddess. And he'd been paying the price for all these years. Now, because of me, he'd pay even longer.

I replayed that moment in the prison over and over in my mind. I'd been right there, ready to release him. I should've done what I knew was right when I'd had the chance. I could've demanded the keys back from Michel. I should have put up a fight, refused to go until *all* the prisoners were released.

The regret and guilt stuck like poison thorns in my side. I had to find him.

It was almost a relief to leave New 2, to get away from the memories, to jump into the mail truck with Crank and drive over Lake Pontchartrain to Covington, the border town, where Bruce and Casey were waiting to meet us.

"You sure you want to do this?" Casey asked me, her arms tight around my neck. She set me back, and I took the moment to memorize her face. Round. Kind. Bright blue eyes that showed every single emotion she had. Eyes that were now brimming with tears.

They knew only that I'd found a strong lead on my father, and I needed to jump on it now before I lost the trail. "I have to do this. I have to find my father."

Bruce was next. He pulled me into a bear hug, into a cloud

of aftershave, a spicy clean mix that made me breathe in deep. I squeezed the soft flannel-clad shoulder. "Take care," he murmured. "Remember your training. We'll expect regular check-ins."

I stepped back and nodded.

"The paperwork won't be final for sixty days, but I guess the Novem has strings, because they sure as hell pulled some to get permission to transfer guardianship," Casey said. "We'll let you know when everything is final."

"Thanks."

Michel Lamarliere would soon be listed as my legal guardian. At least for the next six months, until I turned eighteen.

The Sandersons helped me transfer my belongings from their SUV to the mail truck. I didn't have much—two trash bags full of clothes and shoes, and a couple of boxes with some books and other things I'd collected over the years.

"I put a picture album in one of the boxes," Casey said, fighting back tears.

Bruce shut the back of the truck, and they both wrapped me in another hug. Bruce's voice whispered in my ear. "There's a little something in there from me, too." From the tone of his voice, I'd say it was something of the personal protection variety. "We love you, kiddo."

My throat closed, but I managed to say, "Same here."

As far as good-byes went, this was the hardest. I forced down the rise of tears and kept my composure as we drove away. It was only after Crank had dropped off the mail and retrieved the new bags, and we were headed back down the neglected highway, that I swiped a few tears from the corners of my eyes.

The last rays of the sun spread over the surface of the lake, turning it into a shimmering mirror of deep blues, purples, and oranges. The skyline of New 2 blinked on the horizon, sending me back to the first time Crank and I had driven over the bridge and into the Crescent City. Only this time we didn't head toward the GD. This time we made for the French Quarter.

The truck slowly, and illegally, navigated Royal Street, mindful of the pedestrians and the carriages. Almost dark. Almost time for another Mardi Gras parade and another ball. Things that meant very little to me.

Crank parked outside of the Cabildo. "I'll wait for you here."

I nodded, took a deep breath, put on my game face, and jumped from the truck.

My black boots slapped onto the pavement. The τέρας blade swung against my jeans, secured in a brand-new sheath, with a smaller concealed sheath around my boot that contained Violet's very sharp, very wicked-looking dagger. I was making a statement. I had the blade, and I wasn't keeping it secret. The sides of my hair had been braided and were gathered, with the rest of my hair, into a tight bun at the nape of my neck.

I popped a small bubble with my chewing gum as I opened the thick wooden door and went inside.

The Novem's Council of Nine had gathered.

On the second floor, I ignored the receptionist, one hand resting on the hilt of the τέρας blade, marched down the corridor that held so much history, and crashed the meeting.

Nine faces turned in my direction. Seven of those I'd yet to meet, but from what I'd gleaned from Henri, Sebastian, and the others, I wouldn't have trouble putting the names to the faces.

No one, however, seemed surprised to see me.

Deep breath.

All I had to do was think of Violet, of us laughing and running down First Street in our masks and gowns, of her voice telling me that I was beautiful, of the image of her jumping Athena and stabbing The Bitch in the heart, and I found my strength.

I grabbed a spare chair from the corner and dragged it over the hardwood floor, letting it screech, hoping it'd send chills down the spines of the council members. At the large oval table, I spun the chair around and sat down.

Slowly I met each pair of eyes.

The heads of the three witch families: Lamarliere, Hawthorne, and Cromley. The three vampire families: Arnaud, Mandeville, and Baptiste. And the three demigod/shape-shifter families: Deschanel, Ramsey, and Sinclair.

Another deep breath. Another small bubble popped.

"I'd like to enroll in the Presbytère," I said.

Josephine, in her expensive cream-colored suit, barked a laugh. But no one laughed with her.

After a long moment, Michel spoke up. "I don't see why that should be a problem."

"Of course you wouldn't, Michel. Tell us, Ari, what interest could you possibly have in attending the Novem's school?"

"Well, I'm here to stay. And the way I see it, you need me. All of you need my help. War is coming to New 2."

"We have power," Soren Mandeville said. "And we have enough to protect the city and the people in it."

"In the past, maybe. But this time you have nothing"— my harsh gaze pierced Josephine, promising retribution for the betrayal of my father, for turning him over to Athena when he sought protection within the Novem—"or *no one* to trade for peace."

"We have you," Josephine said quietly.

"Please, Josephine," Rowen Hawthorne said. "We have already agreed to provide sanctuary to Miss Selkirk. We have already fought with Athena and sealed our role in this war. Threatening this young woman is ... redundant."

"You offer to fight, to be part of this battle. And all you want in return is sanctuary and schooling?" Bran Ramsey asked suspiciously.

"I want knowledge." I sat forward, elbows on the table and heart hammering. "I want to learn everything about Athena, the gods, the past, everything there is to know about my curse. I know the Presbytère contains a secret library, one that the students don't even know about. I want access to that, too."

No one spoke, but a few incredulous gasps spread around the room.

"You ask too much," Bran said.

Nell Cromley spoke up, and I couldn't help but wonder if the dark-haired, blue-eyed witch was directly related to the Alice Cromley whose bone I'd ingested into my lungs. "Our knowledge is kept hidden for good reason. Only the nine of us and the translators are permitted within those walls. Our own families do not have access. I am sorry, child, but you are simply too young and inexperienced to grasp what you ask of us. The responsibility that comes with bearing such knowledge is too great."

If only she knew the things I'd had to "bear" in my life already. I hated the implication that I was incapable or irresponsible. *Hated. It.* Frustration ate away at my calm. "Can any of you kill a god?" I glanced around the table. "I mean, really?

Just kill one by standing there and being yourself?" My gaze came back to Nell. "I'll have that power one day. I might have that power now. I don't need your library's knowledge for that. You saw what I did in the cemetery. She's afraid of me."

Michel's lips curled into a small smile, and his gray eyes took on a decisive glint. "I doubt Ari intends on exposing our secrets and our history to the world. Allowing her access to our library and our knowledge only benefits us if the result is Athena's defeat. My son can assist her—"

"Oh, bravo, Michel!" Josephine scoffed. "Bastian is powerful enough."

"And what of our children?" Soren jumped in. "You expect us to agree on *your* son learning the knowledge and not ours?"

"He will be head of this family one day," Michel said. "He will learn it eventually."

"*Oui,*" Soren shot back. "When he takes your place. Then and only then. Just as it is for the rest of us."

Heads nodded around the table. Michel sat back and shrugged. I had to give him props for trying (and for sneaking his son into the library years earlier to show him the Mistborn tablet, something the Novem obviously didn't know about). Now I knew where Sebastian got his tendency to defy authority.

"I would consider this," Nikolai Deschanel said thoughtfully, "if she enters alone, and leaves with nothing. No artifacts, scrolls, or books. No notes, nothing of any kind except what is committed to memory."

"I'd agree to that," I said immediately. I didn't exactly have a photographic memory, but if I found information that helped me locate Athena and Violet, I doubted I'd forget it. And more than anything, I was anxious to get started. "So, what's it going to be? Let me in the school, give me access to the library, and"— I smiled—"I'll take care of your goddess problem."

A few chuckles went around the room.

"But why?" Another Novem head, Simon Baptiste, spoke. "You are a smart young woman. You could hide, disappear from Athena's radar. What could possibly motivate you to do all this, to put yourself in her path and help protect this city? What do you really want? Riches, control, power . . ."

My pulse skipped as my gaze fixed on the powerful vampire. A current of anticipation and conviction snaked through my veins. It was simple.

"I want *vengeance*."

That one single word reverberated through the room as though it held power.

Slowly I leaned back in the chair as the goose bumps on my arms faded.

Vengeance.

I wouldn't stop until I got it. Wouldn't stop until Violet was returned to New 2 safe and sound. Wouldn't stop until my ancestors could rest in peace, and my father was freed. I'd never stop. Not until Athena was dead.

Somewhere in the din of my thoughts I heard them vote. Heard every member echo the word "Aye."

And it was then that I knew, one way or another, no matter how long it took, I'd have my revenge.

Acknowledgments

Much gratitude goes to the amazing folks at Simon Pulse, and to my brilliant editor, Emilia Rhodes. What a fun and exciting journey this has been, and I'm so happy to be working with you!

To the fabulous Miriam Kriss for believing in this book, helping a dream come true, and taking care of business so I could focus on the writing. Thanks for making my writing life infinitely better. It's a pleasure to be your client.

Thanks goes to good friend, fellow author, and CP, Jenna Black, for the read and for being creeped out by portions of this book, to which I responded: *Yes! I have done my job.*

To Kameryn Long, who read the first half of this book in its earliest stage and texted *I hate you!* because I left her hanging. One of the best texts I've ever gotten. Thanks for being my constant champion, Kam.

Big hugs to the Destination Debut girls for all the cheers, commiseration, sharing, and support. Don't know what I'd do without you.

And, as always, to Mom and Dad and my family and friends for the unwavering support, and to Audrey, James, and Jonathan for putting up with my "spacey" moments and allowing me time to dwell in make-believe lands. Thank you for bringing me back down to earth and keeping me grounded.